MURDER ON LAKE STREET

PETER MARABELL

MURDER
ON LAKE STREET

A MICHAEL RUSSO MYSTERY

Amy and Kelly,
who have given me so much

"We know what we are, but not what we may be."

—**William Shakespeare,** *Hamlet*

1

Frank Marshall was shot three weeks ago last night as he left Ristorante Bella in downtown Petoskey. Four shots. Three hits. Two weapons. No witnesses. No suspects. No justice . . . yet.

Reaction was quick and predictable. City Council called a special meeting, the City Manager speculated on what had "gone wrong," and the Chamber of Commerce worried about a slump in business. All of them demanded speedy arrests and tough prosecution at trial.

"You guys are nowhere," I said. "Frank damn near died, and you got nothing. After three weeks?" Marshall, a retired investigator for a powerful Chicago law firm, was my mentor and good friend. Frank Marshall was the closest thing I had to a brother.

"Come on, Russo," Don Hendricks said. Hendricks was the Emmet County prosecutor. We sat in his office, off Lake Street in Petoskey. Hendricks was six-two, two-thirty and rumpled all over. He leaned forward and dropped his elbows on the desk. "We've been on this hard, you know that."

"Not hard enough," I said angrily. "Or you'd have something by now."

"Dammit, Russo," Hendricks said, slapping his large, beefy hand on the desk.

"Gentlemen. Please!" Hendricks and I looked over at Captain Martin Fleener of the Michigan State Police who sat in a walnut high back chair on the sidewall underneath a large, framed map of Emmet County, Michigan. "He's right, Don," Fleener said. "You got no leads, no suspects. Hell, it's my case, and I don't have any leads either."

Fleener shook his head. "But that was a cheap shot, Michael." Fleener stood up. In his forties, he was tall and trim. He took off his suit jacket, a soft gray wool blend with thin red pinstripes, and hung it over the back of the chair. "We all want the guys who did this. Marshall's your friend, but a shooting's bad all around." Fleener sat down again. "Tourists read about it. Locals don't like it. People are nervous. Best if we clear it quickly."

"Didn't have to keep you in this, Russo," Hendricks said, still edgy. "But we did. Wanted you in it from the start."

"We've run a good case, Michael," Fleener said. "You know that."

I looked at Hendricks, then at Fleener. I reached for my coffee mug on Hendricks' desk. "Okay, run it by me."

Hendricks pushed a manila folder across his desk towards Fleener. Hendricks leaned back in his chair, tugged at his loose necktie as if it were too tight. "You do it," he said. Fleener picked the folder up and opened it.

"All right," Fleener said and cleared his throat. "Marshall left Ristorante Bella about 8:30. Alone. After dinner with two friends." Fleener looked up. "Got their statements. Basically, they know nothing." He went back to the folder. "Unless we a got a cowboy with a gun in each hand, we got two shooters because ballistics says we got two guns. A Smith & Wesson .38 and a Tech Nine. Four shots were fired at Marshall. Two from the Nine hit him. One in the left lung, the other nicked his stomach. The third from the .38 just missed his heart. Fourth shot hit the doorjamb of the restaurant. Pretty smashed up." Fleener closed the file.

"That's what you told me the first time," I said.

Fleener nodded.

"Still no witnesses?" I said.

Fleener shook his head. "Lousy night, Michael. Cold rain. Nobody out."

"Nobody?"

"It's October," Fleener said. "Only six other people in the restaurant. No one on the street."

I leaned forward in my chair. "You gonna talk to the restaurant staff again?"

"Three times, Russo," Hendricks said. "Same story each time." He was still edgy. "They knew nothing. They're not involved."

"Who you talking to next?"

"Not sure," Hendricks said. "We'll look at the whole case again."

"Will you email me a copy of the file?"

Hendricks nodded. He reached over, moved a mouse, and clicked it three times. "Done," he said. "Might I be so bold to ask why you need your own copy?" It wasn't a good time for sarcasm.

I stood up, hands on my hips and stared at Hendricks. "Time to run my own case," I said.

"What are you gonna do, counselor?" he said. "Think just because you solved the Abbott murder, you're Spenser for fucking hire?" Summer before last, I helped Hendricks and Fleener find the killer of a wealthy, well-connected aristocrat, Carleton Abbott. I didn't ask for the job, but I put all the pieces together for them. My mentor on that case was Frank Marshall whose current address was intensive care.

"I don't have your legal constraints, Don."

"Michael. Come on," Fleener said. "You're an attorney. You're still an officer of the court."

"Don't get in our way, Russo," Hendricks said.

"Already there, Don," I said. "Time to play it out."

2

left the county building and walked up Lake Street to my office. I zipped my rain parka up tight against the chilly mist. Fall had come quickly to Northern Michigan. After Labor Day, when the tourists are gone, when the heat and humidity are gone, life in Petoskey resumes the leisurely pace of the off-season. The weather, well, sometimes it's sunny and pleasant, sometimes it's all clouds and rain. If the rain hung around, it made people grumpy.

My office was on the second floor of an ornate building on Lake Street in the middle of the Gaslight District. Since I bought the building in 1998, I've slowly restored it, inside and out. Most recently, it got a couple of coats of fresh paint, a soft gray-blue with white trim. My tenant on the street level is Fran Warren, owner of the Mackinac Sandal Company, a shoe business from Mackinac Island.

"Hello, Michael," Sandy said when I walked in the office. "Only two messages," she said, holding up the slips. Sandra Jeffries is part office manager, part assistant. She keeps "Michael Russo, Attorney & Investigations" running smoothly.

"Hello, back," I said. I shook my coat and hung it on the hall tree next to the door.

"Hendricks tell you anything new?" she said.

I shook my head. "Not a thing, I'm sorry to say. You talk to the hospital?"

"I called Ellen before I went to lunch." Ellen Paxton was Frank Marshall's wife and as close a friend to me as Frank. "They moved him out of the ICU into his own room. He's talking more."

"Good to hear," I said. I filled a mug with coffee. "Come in and sit for a minute."

My office was behind Sandy's. It looked out over the parking lot instead of Lake Street, but I had a clear view of Little Traverse Bay two blocks away. The space was a good-sized rectangle with hardwood floors covered in the center by a navy blue and deep red Oriental rug. My desk was a dingy blond monster commandeered from the *Petoskey Post Dispatch* when it remodeled its offices six years ago. Two captain's chairs, one in front of the desk, one on the sidewall were for clients. A large bookcase, stuffed with too many books, filled the other wall.

Sandy sat down. She put down a mug of coffee and handed me a manila folder.

"What's this?"

"Email from Hendricks. The Marshall case file. Figured you'd want a hardcopy."

"You read it?"

Sandy nodded. "Didn't take long," she said. "Not much there. I've read more detail in a Steve Hamilton mystery."

"What do you think?"

Sandy drank some coffee. "Well, if you don't mind me saying so, I can see why Fleener's not getting anywhere. He's got a ballistics report and the crime scene report, and that's about it. Without witnesses, what's he gonna do? He didn't even guess at a motive. How could he?"

"Someone had to see something," I said. "Can't just shoot a man down in the middle of town . . ." I shook my head. "Somebody knows something." I picked up my mug and drank some coffee.

"The only thing I know from the report," Sandy said, "is the cops are looking for two shooters."

I put my mug back on the desk. "Well, it's time we looked for the shooters," I said.

"We, boss?"

"Yes, we."

"So what are we," the "we" came out as one long syllable, "gonna do," Sandy said, "Google 'two shooters' and see who pops up?"

"Smart-ass," I said.

"Thank you."

"But not helpful."

"I know, I know, but Michael, how many angles do we have to work with here?" Sandy said, tapping her right index finger down on the folder. "I mean, Fleener and Hendricks have nothing. Why do you think we can do better?"

"I don't know if we can do better," I said, "but we can do it differently. I can work . . ."

My iPhone chimed. I looked at the screen. It read, "drinks at Chandler's?" It was AJ, Audrey Jean Lester to be precise, my confidante, lover, and partner. She didn't particularly like the label "partner" until I called her "girlfriend." Thought she was gonna smack me on the head. Now she liked "partner" just fine. I tapped, "yes."

"Sorry," I said. "That was AJ." I picked up my coffee. "Now where were we?"

"A different angle to look for the shooters," Sandy said.

"Right," I said.

"What'd AJ want?" Sandy said.

"Meet for drinks after work," I said. "I'll run what little we got by her. Maybe she'll have an idea." AJ was a veteran reporter and editor of *PPD Wired*, the online edition of the *Petoskey Post Dispatch*.

"Michael," Sandy said, "maybe that's a place to start. Not AJ specifically, but the paper. Maury Weston." Weston was editor and publisher of the paper and AJ's boss. "He's been around this town a long time. He's got a reporter's nose for news and for digging stuff up."

"Good idea," I said. "He knows the town, and he can play by different rules than the cops."

"Want me to call him?"

"Yeah. I'll walk over this afternoon if he's got time."

Sandy got up but stopped at the door. "Michael," she said, "one thing worries me."

"And that is?"

"Shooters have guns," she said. "Michael, this is dangerous business."

I reached down, opened the bottom left drawer of my desk. I moved the tape dispenser and brought out a short-barreled Smith & Wesson .38 revolver in a dark brown leather holster and put it on the desk.

Sandy stared at the gun. She nodded, and walked out.

3

I put on my coat and went down the stairs. The mist had let up, but it was still damp and gloomy. I stopped at McLean & Eakin bookstore to get a *New York Times*, then headed up Howard Street for the three-block walk to the *Post Dispatch*. I'll have to postpone an afternoon run until morning since the rest of the day is filled. Besides, the sky is supposed to clear overnight.

Howard Street was busy with traffic, but nothing like it was in mid-July during the peak tourist season. I didn't even have to wait for the light to change to cross at Mitchell. Julienne Tomatoes wasn't busy either, a sure sign that business had slowed until ski season.

The offices of the *Post Dispatch* sit on State Street, in the middle of the block just off Howard. The two-story frame house built in the 1920s resembled others that line city streets all over town, but this one had a large sign in the front yard. A barn red front door and shutters highlighted the white clapboard siding. It was redone years ago to accommodate offices for the paper. Off the back of the house, not easily visible from the street, was a one floor addition filled with more offices and graphic facilities.

I climbed the front stairs and entered the building. Two large rooms went left and right off the central hallway. A staircase went to the second floor and Maury Weston's office.

I said hello to Vickie Stauton at the customer counter in what was the old parlor. Upstairs, I knocked on the doorjamb of Weston's office even though the door was open.

"Come on in, Michael," Weston said. Maury Weston, who became publisher in 2001, was a seasoned reporter and editor. He dragged his six-six-frame out of his chair and came around the desk to shake hands.

"How are you?" he said. Weston wore black wool slacks, a light blue button-down shirt open at the neck and a camel V-neck sweater. "Office casual" had come to the *Post Dispatch*.

Weston's office had been a front bedroom in an earlier life. His cherry desk sat in one corner with a large sash windows to his right. Two brown leather armchairs were at one end of the desk. A large rectangular walnut table with six side chairs dominated the other side of the room.

We shook hands. "I'm fine, Maury," I said. "I appreciate you taking the time to see me."

Sitting in an armchair next to Weston's desk was AJ Lester my, ah, partner. She wore a camel skirt, above the knee, and a black blazer over a white silk blouse. She was a trim five-nine, and her outfit was very appealing. But I thought that every time I saw her.

"Hi," I said, and she smiled back at me.

"I hope I'm not getting in the way of a business meeting."

"Not at all," Weston said. "As soon as I told AJ you wanted to talk about a case, well, you can't keep a good reporter down."

"The more the merrier. I need all the help I can get."

"Have a seat," Weston said, gesturing at the other armchair. "How's Frank doing?"

"A little better. He's in a private room now," I said. "I'll stop by the hospital in the morning."

"Well," Weston said, "what can I do for you?"

"I'm sure you know the cops still have nothing on the shooting."

Weston nodded. "Have you talked with Don Hendricks lately?"

"A couple of hours ago," I said, shaking my head.

"How can I help then?"

"Are we off the record?" I said, looking at AJ, too.

"Do we need to be?" Weston asked. "Are you going to tell me something I'd want to write up for the front page?"

I shook my head. "I hope not."

"Let's do this," Weston said, "our conversation is off the record unless I stop it. That okay?"

"It is." I leaned forward. "I'm gonna find the gunmen who shot Frank Marshall."

"Michael?" It was AJ. "You didn't tell . . . when did you . . ?"

I put my hand on her arm. "It just happened," I said. "An hour ago. Didn't expect to see you until tonight."

"No need to worry about that making the front page, Michael," Weston said.

"Want to keep it quiet best I can," I said. "Don't want whoever did this to get wind that I'm digging, too."

I gave them a short version of my conversation with Hendricks and Fleener.

"They won't make it easy for you, Michael," Weston said.

"I can live with that, Maury," I said. "But I can't live with doing nothing. Frank's too important to me for that."

"Well," Weston said, "I'll ask again, how can I help?"

"I need to know what you know," I said, "or what you've heard on the street. Rumors, gossip, whatever. Gotta start with something the cops don't have or can't use."

Weston leaned back in his chair and put his hands behind his head. He looked at AJ. "You thinking what I'm thinking?" he said.

AJ nodded. "Lenny Stern."

"Uh-huh," Weston said. "Best reporter I've ever seen. A pit-bull who can write." He looked at me. "You know Lenny?"

"Met him a few times. Talked some," I said. "Don't really know him all that well."

"Lenny's lived here most of his life. He knows the good rumors from the bad," AJ said.

"He worked at the paper before I got here," Weston said. "All he ever wanted to be was a reporter."

"Wonder why he didn't go to a big city paper? Chicago or Detroit?"

"He tried that," Weston said.

"Why'd he come back?"

"You'll have to ask him about that," Weston said. "I hope he never retires. Hate to lose him."

"Think he'd talk to me?" I said.

"Let's find out." Weston picked up his cell phone, tapped the screen and waited. "Lenny . . . yeah . . . where are you? Sorry I asked. Uh-huh, yeah . . . listen, Lenny, you know Michael Russo, the . . . yeah, that's him." Weston finished his disjointed conversation. "He'll meet you at the Side Door at five."

"He remember me?"

Weston nodded. "He remembered the Abbott murder, too."

"Everybody does," I said. I stood up and Weston came around his desk. We shook hands. "I appreciate your help, Maury. Thanks."

"You're welcome," he said.

"Stop by the house when you're done with Lenny," AJ said. "I've got fresh salmon."

"You cooking dinner?" I said, surprised.

"No," she said, softly. "I like the way you do it. With dill sauce." I started to laugh but thought better of it.

"Michael," Weston said, "are you sure you want to go after these guys?"

"I'm sure."

"Be careful, you hear?"

4

I got to the Side Door Saloon a little after five. Once you get by the waiting area, which is much too small during the tourist season, the room opens into a big rectangle, with a few dividers to break up the space for tables. The walls are wood and filled with memorabilia and big TVs. A bar wraps around one side of the room by the kitchen. I saw Lenny Stern on a stool at the far end.

"Hello, Lenny," I said, sliding onto the stool next to him.

"Hey, Russo," he said. "How are ya?" We shook hands. Stern was a wiry five-four in his late sixties. He was nearly bald except for some strands of gray that wrapped around the tops of his ears. The rest of the *Post Dispatch* may have switched to business casual, but Stern didn't get the memo. He wore a black, single-breasted suit, a white cotton shirt, not ironed, and a skinny black tie.

"Thanks for meeting me on such short notice."

"No problem," he said, "wanted a beer anyway." Stern looked down the bar. "Johnny," he said to the man behind the bar, "my friend here needs a drink."

"What'll you have?" the bartender said with all the enthusiasm of a guy waiting for the dentist.

"A draft."

He nodded. My beer landed on the bar moments later. I took a long pull and put the glass down.

"Say, Russo," Stern said, "can I ask a question? Before we get to the reason for this little meeting?"

"Go ahead," I said.

Stern drank some beer. "Carleton Abbott," he said.

It'd been more than a year since Abbott's murder at Cherokee Point Resort, just north of Harbor Springs. Sometimes it felt like yesterday.

"You know the killer from the start?"

"Do I look like Sam Spade?"

"You don't even look like Humphrey Bogart," Stern said. "Did you know?"

I shook my head. "If I did, I'd have told the cops and gone back to writing wills and filing divorces."

"What was it then? How'd you figure it out?"

"Just kept digging," I said. "Like a reporter would, Lenny. It just came together, that's all."

Stern nodded slowly. He turned his head my way. "The way I hear it cops remember you helped."

"Yeah, well they're not all that happy with me now."

"Really?" Stern raised his glass in the air, and Johnny came down the bar for a refill. "Tell me."

I did. "That's where you come in," I said. "You know this town, hell, this whole county, as well as anyone. You heard anything that would help? Give me a place to start?"

"Guy gettin' shot's pretty rare. Unless it's deer season." Stern laughed and took a drink of his fresh beer. "If I were on a story, I'd listen to people. Lots of talk about the shooting. One thing I know for sure. It's not a local fight."

"What's that mean?" I said.

"It means Marshall's got no enemies around here. No family grudge match that's boiled over. No problems with money or drugs. No angry husband. The local bad boys don't even know who he is."

"What does that tell you? If you were on this story."

"Look someplace else," he said. "Marshall got shot because he lives here not because the fight's here." Stern tapped my arm. "Want another beer."

"Not right now," I said.

"Where'd Marshall live before he came north?"

"Worked for a big law firm in Chicago. His brother, Tom, was there, too. The University of Chicago."

He smiled. "Nice town," Stern said. "That be a place to start. Maybe a few enemies you don't know about."

"Maybe," I said. I drank the last of my beer and put the glass down. "Lenny, you've covered about everything there is to cover in this town."

"That's for sure."

"How come you never moved up to editor or features?"

"At a desk? Inside?" He shook his head. "I'm the wrong guy for that," he said. "Always have been."

"I hear you worked in Chicago and Detroit. For a big city daily," I said. "Got to be more exciting than Northern Michigan."

Stern laughed. "Sometimes it was," he said and drank some beer.

"Why'd you come back?"

"A woman."

"Is that right?" I said.

He nodded slowly and said. "Story for another time, Russo."

"Well, time for me to get moving anyway," I said.

"I got another question before you go?"

Here comes Cherokee Point or the Abbott killing again. Getting cynical in my old age.

"Cherokee Point."

I zipped my lip. It was hard.

"Only been there once," Stern said. "Beautiful place."

"Yes."

"Strange people," Stern said. "Nasty, arrogant, self-indulgent."

"Yes."

We shook hands. "I appreciate the help, Lenny. Thanks."

"You're welcome."

"Take this, Russo," Stern said. He wrote on the back of a business card. "My cell. Call if you need to."

5

It was a short drive back downtown. I stayed on U.S. 31 as it ran through Bay View. The colors of October and the dark blue water of the Bay made fall an appealing season in Petoskey. But not today. Today was gray and flat. The mist had stopped. That's the best I could say about it. Fall in Northern Michigan.

My apartment building's on Howard Street behind the Perry Hotel. I liked to walk which is a strange comment coming from a car nut who grew up in Detroit. My office is only a block over on Lake, and AJ's house is an easy five blocks up Bay Street. I put my BMW in the parking lot, took my brief bag off the back seat. I shot a quick glance at my latest hot car, grinned like a kid and headed up Bay.

AJ lives in an elegant two-story Victorian overlooking the ravine. It was just far enough from the Gaslight District that few tourists wandered by. The house is white clapboard siding with gray-blue trim on the gingerbread and the windows. She'd carefully restored it inside and out over the years, and it's a comfortable, nurturing home. I went in the back door, off the kitchen.

"Hello, darling," AJ said. I'd just got my coat off when she walked over, put her arms around my neck and kissed me. Hard. I kissed back.

When she pulled away, I said. "Let's do that again." We did. It was just as good the second time.

AJ's black hair was still wet from the shower. It fell in loose curls at the base of her neck. She wore an old pair of green and tan Madras shorts which fit the curves of her backside just tight enough. Her paint-stained gray sweatshirt, with "MSU" in faded green on the front, was way too loose to properly discern the curves of her upper body. I tried anyway.

"Is that beer I smell?"

"Uh-huh."

"When's the last time you had beer?"

"Few minutes ago at the Side Door."

"You're a smart-ass," AJ said. "You know that?"

I smiled. "Seemed like a good idea at the time."

"Well, I'm drinking Chardonnay," AJ said. "Want some?"

"Yes, I do." I opened the refrigerator, got the wine, a block of Horseradish cheese, some crackers and put them on a plate. AJ sat on the couch, an overstuffed piece that could seat four which meant it was long enough that I could stretch out and read a good book. It was upholstered in navy with huge colorful flowers, which matched nicely with the two navy side chairs across from the white wicker coffee table. I put the plate and my wine down. I slipped out of my loafers, sat on the couch next to AJ and put my feet on the coffee table.

"Here's looking at you, blue eyes," I said and we touched glasses.

"My eyes are green," AJ said.

"I know, but I like saying 'blue eyes' better."

AJ snuggled over and I put my arm around her shoulder. "I'm glad you're here," she said. "I missed you this afternoon."

"But I just saw you at Maury's office."

AJ sat up. She cut a piece of cheese and popped it in her mouth without a cracker. "Guess I'm nervous," she said.

"About?"

"About you," she said, "going after the guys who shot Frank."

"I'm sorry I didn't tell you first."

AJ shook her head. "That's not it," she said. "I know you would have told me. It's the fact of it. That you're going to do it."

"The cops have dropped the ball, AJ. This is just another case for them, but I can't get it off my mind. I have this picture of Frank. On the sidewalk, bleeding. In the hospital. He's my closet friend, you know that."

I poured more wine and drank some.

"Last year," I said. "After the Abbott murder."

"I remember," AJ said.

"We'd sit on the porch at his house at Cherokee Point. We'd talk about, well, about being an investigator. How to find out things. How to listen. How to ask questions. It was a tutorial and Frank was the master. I learned from him, but I learned something about myself. He saw that before I did."

"That you could be a good investigator."

I nodded. I looked at AJ, took her hand and kissed it softly. "And now all I can think about is Frank in a hospital bed."

AJ picked up another piece of cheese, but held it in her fingers and pointed at me. "Michael, we both know you won't let this go until the shooters are in jail or in the ground."

I raised my hands, palms up and said, "We'll see."

"We'll see?" AJ said, "don't 'we'll see' me. You sound like my mother." She pointed her finger at me, without cheese, and poked me in the chest. "If I said 'get to the bedroom, I want to jump your bones' would you say 'we'll see?'"

I shook my head. "I'd say, let's go."

"You are a pain in the ass sometimes," she said.

"Only sometimes?"

AJ drank some wine then put her hand on my arm. "I worry about you, Michael. This is dangerous business. Gunning a man down on a public street? People like that won't give up easily."

"I'll be careful," I said. I drank some wine this time.

"I have to admit it," she said. "This last year, you've been pretty conscientious . . ." She laughed, but it wasn't a funny laugh. "Hell, obsessive is a better word, about protecting yourself. Practice at the gun club. The Karate lessons."

"Close to a brown belt," I said.

"If you find these guys, they won't give up easily," she said.

"I will find them."

"Yes." AJ set down her glass and put her head back on my chest. I put my arm around her shoulder and we sat quietly for a time.

"Michael?"

"Hmm."

AJ sat up and looked at me. "I want to jump your bones."

"What about the salmon?"

AJ opened her mouth, but no words came out.

"Hey, I didn't say 'we'll see.'"

AJ grabbed the bottom of her sweatshirt, pulled it over her head and off. She smiled and ran one finger down her left breast to the nipple. "Get to the bedroom. I want to jump your bones."

6

"I'm hungry," AJ said. We were a tangle of arms, legs and warm feelings. Somehow the flannel bed sheet got wrapped under us and around us.

"I thought your hunger would have been satisfied by our voracious lovemaking."

A hand appeared, and AJ pulled the sheet away from her face. "The salmon," she said. "Fix the salmon."

"Can I take a shower first?"

"Yes," she said and yanked the sheet back over her head. I heard a muffled, "Pain in the ass."

I pulled on a pair of black running pants and a faded green "Edina Basketball" sweatshirt. I slipped into black Birkenstock clogs and went out of the bedroom.

By the time AJ arrived in the kitchen, wearing the same shorts and sweatshirt, I'd skinned the salmon and put it in a glass baking dish. I rubbed on a little olive oil, sprinkled Italian spices over the top, and put it in the oven.

"I only found one potato," I said, holding it up. It was easier to find gold in the Yukon than workable items in AJ's pantry or refrigerator.

"One tomato, too," I said and put it on the cutting board. AJ ignored me and poured more wine into our glasses.

"Here's to jumped bones," she said, raising her glass.

AJ took silverware and napkins to a small café table at a window that overlooked the ravine behind her house.

I put a small baked potato and salmon on two plates. I added slices of tomato with a little Fustini's Balsamic dribbled on top and took them to the table.

"Very good, darling," AJ said after her first bite.

"Thank you."

"I forgot to ask about Lenny Stern," she said.

"You had other things on your mind, darling."

"Yes, I did," she said. "Learn anything from Stern?"

I picked up my glass and drank some wine. "Yeah, I did." I told her what Stern said.

"Not local people. Lenny's that sure?"

"He is."

"Then Chicago's worth a look."

"You should be an investigative reporter," I said.

"Very funny. Besides, one of us is enough, darling," AJ said as she cut up her tomato slices.

"More wine?" AJ nodded and I poured the last of the bottle in our glasses.

"Is Frank in any trouble?" AJ said.

I shook my head. "Known him a long time," I said. "Heard plenty of stories about his work in Chicago."

"Like what?" she said.

"Frank tried being a cop for a while," I said. "Didn't pan out. He took a job as the in-house investigator for an influential Michigan Avenue law firm. He did background checks on some powerful people, some of whom were in big trouble. Embezzlement, fraud, arson."

"Powerful enough to hurt Frank?"

I shook my head. "Don't know for sure, but nothing sticks out."

I finished the last of my salmon and pushed my plate aside. "But it deserves a look. No one knows the landscape in Emmet County like Lenny."

"Better than the cops? Or the prosecutor?"

"Not necessarily better," I said. I drank the last of my wine. "Fleener and Hendricks are good at what they do, but people talk to Lenny. Lots of contacts. Hears things the cops won't."

"Don't you think Marty Fleener'd thought of Chicago? I mean, with no leads here?"

"Yeah, I do. Maybe Fleener hasn't asked Frank yet. He's only been awake and talking a few days."

"Are you still going to the hospital in the morning?" AJ said.

I nodded. "First thing. Then to the office."

"You gonna stay with me tonight?" She reached over took my hand in hers.

"Thought I might."

"Want me to take my sweatshirt off again?"

"You'd do that anyway when we go to bed," I said.

"Un-huh, but that's not what I meant."

"Oh."

7

I woke up a little after eight. I slipped out of bed, grabbed my clothes and dressed in the bathroom. I decided not to wake AJ just to just to say good-bye. I went down Howard, cut through the parking lot of the Perry Hotel to my apartment building.

I took a shower while the coffee brewed. I added a dark green blazer to my standard-issue khakis just to be daring. Good enough for the office or for this morning's stop at the hospital.

It was still chilly, still damp and the gray sky promised rain soon. If I had time this afternoon, I badly wanted to get a run in. It'd been three days, and I was itchy for some exercise. I often did my best thinking on a pleasant run through the streets of Bay View or on the hills of Mackinac Island.

I resisted the temptation to stop at Johan's for two glazed donuts since it was across the street from the hospital. I knew a lot of the staff after three weeks of regular visits. And the three Sheriff's deputies who rotated shifts not far from Frank's room. Two donuts, just for me? Couldn't be that rude to people watching out for Frank.

"Don't remember much," Frank Marshall said from his bed. "Happened so fast." He waked up suddenly, talked some, tried to move, then went back to sleep.

"I glad he's in his own room," Ellen Paxton said. "He's doing a lot better." Paxton was a retired Chicago stockbroker. She lived with Marshall in an elegant, three story Victorian cottage at Cherokee Point Resort on Lake Michigan, north of Harbor Springs. Paxton was at her husband's bedside when he woke for the first time.

I was there, too.

"He wakes up more often now," she said. "Stays awake longer." Ellen got out of the chair and stretched her arms up, over her head. "Feel like I'm glued to that chair," she said. She turned and looked out the window. The Bay was only a block away. "No rain yet," she said.

"I'll sit with Frank if you want to go ride." Ellen was an avid bike rider, often using the hills of Petoskey or taking the trail down through Bay Harbor and Charlevoix to Traverse City to stay in shape. Nothing about her appearance tipped off that, like her husband, she was in her late sixties. Her soft blond hair had only recently started to turn gray. Standing about five-five, she was a trim one-fifteen, and wore jeans well enough to be the envy of many a thirty year old.

"A few more days," she said. "Then I'll accept your offer."

"Deal."

Frank moved an arm and scratched his face. He looked up, first at Ellen then at me. She bent over and kissed him on the cheek.

"Hi, Michael," he said.

I reached out and took his hand. "How you feeling?"

"Better, I think." He moved his other arm from under the covers. His face was thinner and pale, but his eyes were more alert than just moments ago. "Was I talking about something?"

"Ristorante Bella," I said.

Frank nodded slowly. "Can't tell you any more than I told Fleener," Marshall said. "Wish I could." He winced as he moved his right leg to one side of the bed. "Walked out of the restaurant. That was it," he said, "until I saw your sorry faces staring at me." Marshall looked at each of us. Then, he was asleep again.

"Want coffee?" Ellen said, pointing towards the door.

We took the elevator to the first floor and went into the cafeteria. We got coffee from a large stainless steel urn and went to a table on the far wall, away from the door. It was quieter. I swallowed some coffee. It wasn't very good or very strong.

Ellen chuckled. "At least it's coffee," she said.

"If you say so." I took another drink. It didn't help.

We sat quietly for a time. Ellen was weary and tired, but she was more relaxed this morning than any time since the shooting.

I leaned forward, arms on the table. "Probably shouldn't have been so hard on Hendricks," I said. Ellen shrugged. "But those guys ought to have something by now."

"Damn right, they should," she said, suddenly angry.

"Hendricks and Fleener are good," I said. "Don't underestimate them because this is a small town."

Ellen shook her head. "I don't. I have great respect for both of them. So does Frank, but . . . nothing?" She picked up her coffee, but put the cup back on the table without a drink. "They got too many cases? Not enough time? What? A shooting's bad for the town. That ought to get their asses in gear." She was still angry. "Why isn't it done, Michael? Tell me. Why goddamn it?"

"I don't know, Ellen," I said.

"This is personal for you and me, Michael."

I nodded.

"You're closer to him than anyone else."

I nodded again.

"You have to get those guys," Ellen said.

"Yes," I said. "It's time. I'll find them, Ellen."

"Good," she said. "I'll help anyway I can."

"Hire me."

"What?"

"Hire me to look into the shooting of your husband," I said. "Make it official. Pay me. Then I'm not obliged to tell Fleener anything. He can ask, but that's all he can do."

"You think that's important?"

"Yeah," I said. "I'm gonna do things the cops can't do. Don't want pressure to talk about it."

"Okay, you're hired." Ellen reached down and picked up her brown Coach bag and took out a checkbook. "The retainer," she said. "How much?"

I told her.

"One dollar? Be serious, Michael."

"I am serious, but make it a hundred dollars, if you'll feel better."

She nodded and wrote the check. "Here," she said.

"Thanks. I'll have Sandy draw up the contract. Now it's official. I work for you."

"So when do we start?"

"You know Lenny Stern?" I asked.

"The reporter? Looks like he just stepped out of a stage version of *The Front Page*?"

I laughed. "Yep, that's him." I told Ellen what Stern told me.

"You think he's right?" she said.

"At first, I did," I said. "Then I thought about it. Cops went through all the files in his office, right?" Ellen nodded. "The Chicago ones, too? And the old ones in storage?" She nodded again. "Nothing. Not a thing." I went for my coffee cup, but it was empty.

"Want some more coffee?" I said to Ellen. She shook her head. The cafeteria was busy with staff and visitors. Most of the tables were filled and about ten people waited quietly in line for food.

"I went through most of it," I said. "His computer, too. The files in his desk. Nothing."

"It's not in the files," Ellen said.

"What?"

"Never was."

"What are you talking about?"

Ellen rubbed her eyes and her voice softened. "I've been so worried about Frank these last few weeks," she said. "I didn't think about other things until I knew he'd be okay. That's when it hit me."

"What did?"

Ellen leaned forward, closer to me.

"It's just a theory, you understand, but my gut tells me . . ."

"Tells you what?" I said.

"It's not in the files because Frank kept it off the books. He was on his own time, even though the firm helped him with background work and time off."

"I'm listening."

"About twenty years ago, '93, I think, or '94, Frank's brother, Tom had big trouble. Ever meet Tom?"

I shook my head. "Heard a few stories."

"We haven't seen Tom in years. Not sure if Frank even knows where he is." Ellen scratched her forehead. "The brothers had a pretty easy life as kids. Family money, nice house in Birmingham, good schools. Frank built a nice life for himself. But Tom never really grew up. He behaved like an entitled sixteen year-old most of the time even though he had a successful career."

"Wasn't he a teacher?"

"Un-huh," she said. "The University of Chicago. Professor of History." Ellen looked out, over the room. Her thoughts took her away for a moment.

"Anyway, Tom had a torrid affair with the wife a Mafia tough guy. His name was Rick Morgan. The wife was Clare Morgan."

"A college professor and the mob?"

"Un-huh," Ellen said. "Tom was in the affair, then said he wasn't. He was screwing her, then said he'd stopped. On and on. Frank tried to talk to him, but Tom wouldn't listen. He sounded like a high school kid who only thought about sex."

"You're not making this up, are you?"

Ellen shook her head. "Tom and Clare ran off to Paris and took a suitcase full of her husband's money with them. Morgan tried to kill Tom."

I rolled my eyes. "Well, Paris is a nice place to die if you're writing a suspense novel."

"Except it's not fiction," Ellen said.

"No, it's not."

Ellen nodded and sat back in her chair.

"Frank got beat up one night by Morgan and one of his goons."

"Two on one? Hurt bad?" I said.

"Bad enough, but Frank evened the score. There was payback."

"Tough man," I said.

"Tougher than you know, Michael."

Ellen leaned forward again, resting on her elbows, and stared at her coffee cup.

"To make a long saga mercifully shorter, Frank engineered a deal to keep Tom alive. Morgan got most of the money back, but Clare wanted out the marriage. Morgan didn't like the idea, but he didn't have much choice. Frank always thought Morgan blamed him because he put the deal together."

"You think the shooting's tied to Chicago twenty years ago?"

"Can't prove it, but yes," she said. "Must be some way to find Morgan. Find out about him and his ex-wife."

"There's always a way," I said. "I don't know, Ellen, you really think two wiseguys from the Windy City came all the way up here just to kill Frank?"

"If they were ordered to," Ellen said. She hesitated. "Remember, it's just a theory."

"Well," I said, "it's better than no theory at all."

Ellen looked at her watch. "I want to get back upstairs, Michael," she said. "Come on, I'll walk you out."

We left the table and went to the lobby.

"Let me think on it," I said. "I'll need more information on, ah, what were the names again?"

"Morgan. Rick and Clare Morgan," Ellen said. "I've got my iPad upstairs. I'll write you an email when Frank's asleep."

I nodded. "See you tomorrow, then." I turned to leave.

"Michael?"

I stopped and looked back. Ellen walked over and kissed me on the cheek. "Be careful. Ask too many questions, those guys might come back to kill you."

7

I came out the hospital parking lot onto U.S 31, went up Mitchell, then left on Howard. I'd never try that in July, but in October cars actually move freely on the downtown streets. I pulled into the parking lot behind my building and slid into my assigned spot.

I dropped my brief bag at the door, and called Sandy.

"Morning, boss. Where are you?"

"Hi, Sandy," I said. "Gonna be late this morning . . ."

"You're already late this morning," she said.

"Being a smart-ass awful early, aren't you?"

"Easy to do in your case," she said. "What's going on?"

"Just saw Frank and Ellen. Going for a run, then I'll be in."

"Your only appointment's at three," Sandy said, "so take your time. I'm ordering a sandwich at Roast & Toast, want anything?"

"Get me a Denver egg wrap."

I clicked the phone and put it on the kitchen counter. Inside a closet by the front door was a small two-drawer chest filled with running gear. The clammy fall weather hadn't eased up, so I got out wind pants, a white long-sleeve T that said, "MSU Spartans" on the front, and my Brooks shoes.

Outside, I ran slowly to Rose Street and loosened up on my usual route up Arlington. By the time I got to Bay View Association, I was moving at a good pace. Once Labor Day is behind us, the streets of Bay View empty out quickly. With fewer cars to worry about, my head focused on Frank, the shooters and Chicago. Somebody gets shot, it's usually about sex, money or revenge. No good-looking women have shown up at the office. Not yet anyway. No suitcase full of cash either. So it must be about getting even.

I turned on Knapp and headed to Glendale. Start with Rick Morgan. Where is he? He'd be in his seventies it he didn't get bumped off. Wife'd be about the same age. Their children'd be adults by know, if they had children.

When I got to Encampment Avenue, I flipped around and headed home. Can't just do a Google search for bad guys in Chicago and hope to learn anything. Back on Arlington, I picked up the pace the last mile. Going for a gonzo finish. Breathing hard.

Petoskey is good for runners, but Mackinac Island is paradise. Gotta get back there before the ferries quit running from Mackinaw City at the end of the month. I clicked off my watch. After sixty minutes of thinking, I knew where to start.

Time to visit Mackinac Island.

Time for a good October run through the hills and history in the middle of the Island. And time to see Carmine DeMio. Trying to find an old-time mobster from Chicago? Who better to ask than a retired Mafia don from the Windy City who just happens to live on the Island's East Bluff in the summer.

I walked around for a few minutes to cool down then went inside for a shower. Hadn't thought about Carmine DeMio in more than a year. Joey DeMio, Carmine's son who took over the family business, was arrested and charged with the murder of Carleton Abbott at Cherokee Point Resort. I proved Joey didn't kill Abbott by proving who did. Carmine expressed his gratitude by offering me a favor that I could call in at any time. Never thought seriously about it. Until now.

I drank a second bottle of water while I shaved and got dressed. With a client coming in this afternoon, I added a navy blazer to my khakis and blue shirt. Very professional for tourist country.

I walked up Howard and cut through the parking lot to McLean & Eakin to get my *New York Times*.

"Good morning, Mr. Russo," Nancy said from behind the counter. "Here's your *Times*."

"Thanks," I said. "Did you get the new Aaron Stander mystery yet?"

"Two weeks, maybe three."

I asked her to save me a copy and headed out the door.

"Hello, Michael," Sandy said when I got to the office.

"You eat yet?"

"Nope. Waiting for you," Sandy said. "Your messages and the Denver wrap're on your desk. Bottle of water, too."

"Thanks," I said. I took off my rain jacket and hung it on the hall tree at the door.

"Ooh, pretty snappy outfit, boss," Sandy said. "A little preppy, even without a tie, but professional enough. For up here."

"Would Diane von Furstenberg grab her sandwich and come in the office."

We settled in at my desk and ate food. "Wanted to dress up a bit since a new client's stopping by today."

"Good thing, too," Sandy said, unwrapping her Avocado Veggie sandwich. "We could use the money."

"Don't remind me," I said. "Who's the client, again?"

"Name's Pamela Wiecek. The file's right there," Sandy said, pointing to a manila folder on the corner of the desk.

I opened the folder. "There's nothing in here. Just a name on the tab."

"She hasn't been here yet. Figured you'd start the file when you talk to her."

"How do you pronounce the name," I said looking at the folder.

"Like checkmate," Sandy said. "Pamela 'we-check.'" She bit off a chunk of sandwich. "Pretty tasty. How's the wrap?"

"Always a good choice," I said. "Did she say why she needed a lawyer?"

Sandy shook her head. "A 'personal matter.' That's all she'd tell me."

"Oh, that," I said.

"Un-huh."

We ate quietly for a few moments. I'd eaten half of my Denver wrap when Sandy said, "What's new at the hospital?"

I updated her on Frank's condition and recounted my conversation with Ellen.

"She okay with you going after the shooters?"

"More than okay," I said. "She wants me to do it. She's pretty angry."

"Got a right to be."

I nodded. "Angry at the bad guys. Angry at Fleener. Probably angry at Frank for scaring the daylights out of her for not being more careful."

"How do you be careful about something twenty years ago? If Ellen's right, I mean."

"Don't know," I said. "I have to do more, that's all."

"You are, Michael," Sandy said. "She has to work through the fear herself, but you've been there for both of them since this happened. And now, going after the shooters . . . you're doing a lot."

"Hope so," I said. We finished our food and cleaned up the desk. I drank more water while Sandy got a mug of coffee.

"Is it really possible this started in Chicago twenty years ago?" Sandy asked, and drank some coffee.

"Place to start," I said. "Ellen's gonna email me some information about Rick Morgan. Be sure to read it."

"Will do," she said.

"Next thing we do is find Rick Morgan."

"Want me to try 'oldwiseguys.com' and see what pops?"

"I'll let that go," I said. I leaned back in my chair and put my hands behind my head. "Besides, I got a better idea. Not funnier, but better."

"And that is?"

"Carmine DeMio. Man owes me a favor, remember?"

Sandy nodded. "I do remember," she said with a big smile. "I could call his secretary, what's his name, ah . . ."

"Carlo Vollini."

"Right. Vollini. Guy with the five pack-a-day voice. Want me to get you an appointment with DeMio?"

"Mackinac Island's always a good place to start everything," I said. "Make the call."

8

"**M**ichael?" Sandy said, from the doorway. "Ms. Wiecek is here."

"Send her in," I said, and came around from behind my desk.

Sandy stepped aside and in walked a woman in her late twenties about five-six with flat brown hair, parted in the middle and cut straight across in the back. Her face was round, but not heavy and she had no makeup on that I could tell. She wore a black V-neck sweater over a tan skirt. She handed her rain parka to Sandy, and we shook hands. "Have a seat," I said, pointing to the client chair in front of the desk.

"Michael," Sandy said, "Ellen's email arrived."

I nodded, and Sandy closed the door.

"Thank you for seeing me, Mr. Russo," Pam Wiecek said.

I leaned forward with my arms on the desk. "Ms. Wiecek," I said, "how can I help you?"

"Well," she said, "I have a problem. I don't know what to do about it."

"Okay."

"I mean I have to do something. I just don't know what." Wiecek crossed and uncrossed her legs. Twice. She stared at something in the air. Not at me. Not out the window. She held on to the arms of the captain's chair like she'd fall to the floor if she didn't.

"Okay," I said again. This was going well.

"But Fran Warren thought you could help," Wiecek said. "I know her from the Island."

"Fran's a good friend," I said.

"She said that, yes." Wiecek hesitated. "Anyway . . ."

"How can I help?" I said, trying to be, well, helpful.

Wiecek cleared her throat, leaned forward in her chair. "I want you to find my sister. Her name's Laurie."

I moved a yellow pad closer and picked up a pencil. Might actually have something to write down. "Same last name?" Wiecek nodded.

"How long's she been missing?" I asked.

"About three weeks."

"Have you gone to the police?"

Wiecek shook her head. "Laurie's not really missing," she said. She shook her head again. "Maybe I should start over."

"Why don't you tell me what happened. From the beginning." I sounded like a crime novel.

"She ran off with a guy from work. No good, but she fell for him." Wiecek rearranged herself in the chair. "We work seasonal jobs, Laurie and me. Have for years. We share an apartment near Pellston. Started on the Island in May. Horn's Bar. Laurie got fired in June. Drank too much, always late for her shifts. Anyway, she got a job at Bernie's in Mackinaw City. You know it?"

"Run down place over by the Marathon station?"

"Uh-huh. That's where she met Eddie."

"Last name?"

"Garner. Eddie Garner. Drugs, booze. Bad man, but she wouldn't listen to me. Both of 'em got fired the week after Labor Day. Took off the week after that. Laurie left a note that said, 'I love Eddie.' That's all. I want you to find her."

"Think she might come home?"

"Not sure," she said. "I'm really worried about her. She could end up in real trouble if she stays with Eddie very long. Can't be far away. Eddie's too stupid to think much beyond Northern Michigan."

"I could ask around," I said.

"How much do you charge?" I told her. She took a checkbook from her purse and handed me two photographs and a sheet of paper. "Places we worked, manager names, stuff like that. Keep the pictures." She wrote out a check on the corner of the desk and gave it to me. "That enough?"

"Yes, thank you," I said. "Where can I find you?"

"My cell number's on the bottom of the check. Working at Audie's in Mackinaw City for the winter. In the bar. You can find me there."

I stood up and came around the desk. "Give me a few days. See what I can dig up and I'll get back to you."

"Thank you," she said. We shook hands, and she left the office.

Sandy watched Wiecek leave. "Paying client?"

I handed her the check. "Solid gold."

"At least it's a local bank," she said and put it in the top drawer of her desk.

"You read Ellen's email?" I said, filling a mug with coffee.

"I did."

I walked to the window that looked out on Lake Street. Not many cars parked on the street. Not many people walking around either. It's October, after all. I leaned against the window ledge.

"What do you think?" I said.

"What do I think about a Mafia princess who hooks up with a History professor?"

"Yeah," I said, "and the whole sorry tale."

"Words fail me," she said.

"Bullshit. Words never fail you, Sandy."

"It'd make a bad novel and a worse movie," she said. "But as a motive for a twenty year grudge? Why not. Pretty strange fucking world sometimes."

I nodded. "Yeah, I'm sad to say."

"Ellen didn't say much about Tom after Paris," I said. "Anything about that in the email?"

"Not much," Sandy said. "Frank's not heard from him in years." She held up the email. "There's more here. Names, phone numbers. Stuff like that." She handed me the copy.

"Ellen's pretty sure about this. Guess it's time to look up Rick Morgan." I put my mug down. "Did you get a time with DeMio?"

"His secretary'll call me back."

I looked at my watch. "Gotta meet AJ," I said. "See you in the morning."

9

Chandler's is up Howard from my office, tucked in a courtyard behind Symons General Store. It's a small rectangular space, filled with tables and a bar on the left. AJ sat on a stool talking with Jack, the bartender, a small, narrow man with short salt-and-pepper hair. He saw me first.

"Michael," he said.

"Jack. How are you this evening?"

"Doing fine, Michael," Jack said. "Slow night." Only two tables were filled. A six-top in the back, men and women in their thirties, was making some noise and enjoying themselves. A couple at a two-top near the door was quietly talking, also enjoying themselves, but in a more affectionate way.

I put my arm around AJ's shoulder and kissed her on the cheek.

"That Chardonnay?"

AJ nodded.

"Me, too, Jack," I said. "And a glass of water, please."

"Be right back," he said.

AJ put her arm through my arm, as if we were walking down the street. "I missed you today," she said. "Don't know why. Just wanted to give you a big hug all day."

Jack put down a coaster, my wine and some water.

I raised my wine glass toward AJ, and said, "Here's to hugs."

"Here, here," she said, clinking my glass.

"Should I order a cheese plate?"

AJ nodded.

"Jack?" The bartender came our way. I ordered the appetizer.

"I assume you talked to Frank and Ellen about Chicago," AJ said.

"This morning, but just Ellen," I said. "She thinks we're on the right track." I told AJ about the Morgans, Tom, and the affair.

"Pretty wacky," she said, "nobody'd ever write a novel like that."

"Sandy said the same thing, but Ellen seems convinced."

"Revenge? After all these years? Boy, I dunno, Michael."

Jack put napkins and a plate of cheeses in front of us. "Enjoy," he said. I took a chunk and popped in my mouth.

"It's a place to start, that's all," I said, trying to talk and chew at the same time.

"So you have to find Morgan," AJ said. "You going to Chicago? Maybe Frank still has contacts there."

"Going to Mackinac Island first. Wanna come?"

"I love the Island, you know that, but shouldn't . . . why are you shaking your head, Michael?"

I picked up a cracker, added cheese and smiled at AJ.

"Don't give me that shit-eating grin. Just tell me."

"Carmine DeMio."

AJ opened her mouth slightly then closed it. She nodded. "It takes a gangster to find a gangster. Always knew you were sharp, Michael."

"Thank you, darling," I said. "Man knows a lot of people in the Windy City."

"Or he knows people who would know."

"Can you get away from work and come with me?"

AJ drank some wine. "Yes, I can do that."

"Wasn't that long ago when getting away was almost impossible."

"Well," AJ said, "I think we got *PPD Wired* working smoothly. At least for now." When AJ took over the electronic edition of the paper more than a year ago, it needed a complete overhaul. "It gets a lot of hits for a small town. That's the good news. Now we spend time debating a fee for the online edition. Or how much social media will help create interest in the online edition. Stuff like that."

She leaned over, put her face close to mine, and said softly, "The better news is I'd be happy to go to the Island with you."

"Overnight?"

"Ooh, do you have something romantic planned?" AJ said, touching my earlobe with her fingers.

"I was thinking sleazy."

"Sleazy it is," AJ said and raised her glass. "When are we going?"

"I got a text from Sandy on the way over," I said and drank the last of my wine. "I meet with Carmine tomorrow afternoon." I looked at my watch. "It's early enough, I'll call the Cloghaun and get a room." The bed and breakfast on Market Street was one of our favorite places.

"They haven't closed yet?"

I shook my head. "The 'Great Turtle Weekend' isn't until the end of the month." The last big weekend of the season combined a half-marathon and Halloween trick-or-treating into three days of family fun. "They're still open," I said.

AJ put an arm around my shoulder. "Come to my house and help me pick a sleazy outfit or two for the trip. I'll model several choices."

"You mean I get to pick?"

"No, but you can ogle while I do the picking."

10

I tried to move my right arm, it was stuck under AJ's shoulder and the blanket. It didn't want to budge. I tried again. AJ mumbled something.

"I'm stuck," I said, "move over." With one eye barely open I could see the mound of blankets move. "Not my way. The other way."

"Okay," she said. "Do we have to get up?"

"It's almost seven," I said. "Have to head home."

"Hmm," she said. "I'll stay here for a while."

I got out of bed, picked up my clothes off the floor and took them into the bathroom. I came back out, kissed AJ on the cheek, and said, "I'll make coffee on my way out. Call you later."

"Hmm," she said. "Okay."

The sky was light enough to see there were no clouds in the sky. The air was chilly, but we'd get a drier, sunny day for a change. I went down Bay Street toward the water. AJ's house is a four block walk from my apartment. I cut behind the Perry Hotel and in the back door of my building.

I've lived in this two-bedroom place since I moved North in 1998. It has a comfortable late 1940s feel with plaster walls painted a soft almond and real wood moldings around the doors and windows. The rooms are small by today's standards, but I have a decent view of the Bay. Never found anything I liked better. And I can walk anywhere I need to go downtown.

I put coffee on, took a shower, and drank some while I packed for our overnight on Mackinac. I couldn't shake an uneasy feeling about meeting Carmine DeMio this afternoon. Didn't expect trouble, but something bothered me. Not sure what.

I got out a fresh pair of khakis, pleated, jeans, two blue shirts, a navy crewneck sweater and some underwear. It all fit in my bag with a selection of gear for a fall run on the Island.

I put the bag in the car and went to the office.

"Good morning, Michael," Sandy said. "Mail's not here yet, two messages are on your desk."

"Thanks," I said. I hung up my coat and filled a mug with coffee.

"Michael, I have to take dad to the doctor this afternoon." Sandy lived in a small house on Crooked Lake, just north of town. She moved in to care for her father after her mother died. "I'll work through lunch and leave about two."

"Okay," I said.

"You have two appointments, both this morning. Nothing new. Files are on your desk." Sandy followed me in my office. "I assume you're going to meet our favorite gangster."

I nodded. "Going up with AJ this afternoon and stay overnight. Which reminds me, I gotta check the ferry schedule."

"Want an update on the Mackinac Mafia, too?" she said on the way out.

"Sandy."

"Just kidding," she said, "just kidding."

I checked the ferry brochure, swiped the screen on my iPhone and sent AJ a text, "your house 3:30." I resisted the temptation to include a face blowing a kiss.

I leaned back in my chair and opened the file on my first client of the day.

Three hours, one Turkey Club sandwich from Roast & Toast, and two mugs of coffee later, I'd said good-bye to my second client of the day, when I heard heavy feet on the stairs. The door opened and Marty Fleener came in. He hung his Burberry coat on the rack at the door. Always the impeccable dresser, Fleener wore a single-breasted dark gray worsted suit. Very nice.

"Michael, we need to talk," and pointed at my office. He went in and dropped himself in the client chair.

I took my usual seat, put my feet up on the corner of the desk, and said, "So?"

"So . . . what have you found out about the gunmen?"

I put my hands up, behind my head. And waited.

"Well?"

"Well, what?" I said.

Fleener crossed his legs. "We could trade," he said.

A trade? Bet he had nothing to trade.

"Okay," I said, "you first."

"Michael. Come on. This isn't a game."

My feet hit the floor and I leaned on the desk. "Damn right it isn't," I said. "You want what I know? You want to trade 'cuz you don't know anything? What have you got to trade?"

Fleener shrugged. "Nothing much," he said. I talked with Frank and Ellen. Couple of new details. That's all."

I wonder why they didn't tell him about Rick Morgan or Chicago?

"Look, Marty, we've known each other a long time. Work together sometimes, sometimes not. Don't care which this time. I will find those guys."

"Hendricks is still pissed at you from the other day," he said.

"His problem."

"It'll be your problem you get in the way."

"In the way of what, Marty?" I said, sharply. "Not much to get in the way of."

Fleener waited a moment then got out of the chair, picked up his coat, said, "Be seeing you," and left the office.

That went well. Keeping the cops happy wasn't my job, but there had to be a reason why they have no leads. Had to be a reason why neither Frank nor Ellen told Fleener about Morgan and revenge.

11

I got the 335 from the parking lot, drove up Bay Street and pulled into AJ's driveway. She must have been watching because she came right out the door and down the front steps.

"Hi, sweetheart," she said. "I'm excited about our mini-vacation."

"Me, too."

I went to U.S. 31 north for the fifty minute ride to Mackinaw City. We rode quietly most of the trip, listening to Interlochen public radio.

"Nervous about your meeting?"

"Yeah," I said. "Have been since this morning. Still can't figure out why." Traffic was light, even through Alanson.

"Could be you're excited," AJ said.

"Huh?"

"I'm playing shrink here, but the flip side of fear is excitement. You haven't done much lately besides wills, divorces, that kind of thing. Now you're investigating a shooting. You're back to the mob on Mackinac Island."

"Yeah, yeah, but DeMio's just helping out this time."

"It's exciting stuff for you. I'm just saying."

"Can I get back to you on that for our next appointment, doctor?" I said sarcastically.

"It's on the couch the next time, buster."

"Promise?" I said and put my hand on her thigh.

"Manual transmission, Russo," AJ said. "Put your hands where they belong."

We arrived at the Shepler's parking lot with little time to spare. We bought tickets and went aboard the Wyandot. It was less than half full. Mostly commuters.

"Michael?" AJ said as we crossed the Straits of Mackinac, the Mackinac Bridge on our left. A magnificent sight even on a dull, gray day.

"Yeah?"

"I wish you could see your face," she said. "You're like a kid on Christmas morning. That first glimpse of the tree." AJ was right. I never tired of the bridge, the Straits, or the harbor on the island. It stirred my soul, won my heart.

"You're like this every time."

"Can't help it," I said.

"Don't ever lose that, Michael," she said. "It's charming. It's part of why I love you."

"You're very sweet," I said and leaned over and we kissed. "Thank you."

"The Woods closed last week," AJ said. "How about we get sandwiches downtown?"

"Deal."

The Wyandot cut its engines as we came into the marina and edged our way to the dock.

"Look," AJ said, pointing to a man standing near the ramp. "It's Henri." Henri LaCroix was a friend to both of us. A trained and hardened six-three and 230, he was half-brother to Fran Warren, of Mackinac Sandal Company fame. He wore jeans, a black turtle neck sweater and a tan Carhartt Chore coat. Zipped. His jacket was always zipped.

AJ waved through the window. Henri smiled and waved back. We waited for the deckhands to move the luggage carts and went up the ramp.

"Henri," AJ said, giving him a big hug.

"AJ, Michael," he said, "good to see you both."

"You headed to the City?"

Henri nodded. "Got a few errands," he said. "Be back on the six-thirty."

"I wondered if you might be here to meet us." AJ said.

"No need. He's just meeting DeMio," Henri said. "Russo can probably handle that."

"What about Cicci and Rosato?" I asked. Santino Cicci and Gino Rosato were DeMio's tough guys. They went where he went. They made trouble when he told them to.

Henri shook his head. "They won't bother you this time."

"You knew we were coming?" AJ said.

"Of course."

"We're at . . ."

"The Cloghaun," Henri said. "I know."

"Is Fran on the Island?"

He shook his head. "Traverse City. Back tomorrow, I think."

"We could have coffee in the morning," I said.

"Have to go. I'll find you in the morning," he said and went down the ramp.

We walked to Main Street to get our bags.

"Think Henri's wearing his gun under that coat?" AJ said.

"Count on it."

12

We took our bags off the luggage cart and went up Hoban to the Cloghaun Bed & Breakfast. The two-story gleaming white Victorian house sat at the top of the hill on Market Street. A balcony stretched across the second floor, as did a porch for guests on the first floor. Colorful mums had been added to the plants and flowers that still filled beds in the front yard. We went up the stairs and inside.

"Mr. Russo, Ms. Lester," the woman at the desk said. "Welcome back to the Cloghaun."

"Thank you," I said.

"You're all set. Top of the stairs, room two, in front," and she handed us each a key.

"That the one with the big claw-foot tub?"

"That's the one," she said.

We thanked her and went upstairs. I dropped my bag on the floor next to the bed, a four-poster with a canopy. AJ went out on the balcony. I followed.

"Chilly up here," she said. I came up from behind and wrapped my arms around her. "Warmer already," she said. We looked straight down Hoban Street.

"Let's go to the 'VI' for dinner," AJ said gesturing at the sign for the Village Inn half way down the block.

"Okay," I said.

AJ turned and put her arms around me and we kissed. Gently at first, then hard. I pulled her to me tight. "Ooh," she said.

"Could be late for my meeting," I said.

"Don't want to piss off the mob, darling, especially since you're the one who needs help."

"Good point," I said.

"You really think DeMio will help you?"

"Good chance of it," I said. "He could have said no to the meeting, after all."

"He could be curious why you called in the first place," AJ said. "But he's as connected in Chicago as you can get."

I went inside and exchanged my crewneck sweater for navy blazer.

"Darling?"

"What?"

"You look very sexy in the blazer. Wear it to dinner."

"You said I always looked sexy."

"Go talk to the mob, will ya?" AJ said. "I'm going for a walk while you're gone. I'll take a quick bath before dinner."

"Take your bath after dinner," I said and picked up my coat.

"Why?"

"So I can watch."

AJ raised her arm and pointed at the door. "Out."

I went down Market Street, Back Street it's sometimes called, passing City Hall and the Post Office. I cut across the park, in front of Fr. Marquette's statue, and on to the circle drive at the Marquette Park Hotel.

13

Carmine DeMio bought the Victorian building that became his hotel in 1998. All four stories featured windows, balconies and white paint with black trim. He worked out of an office in the back, off the lobby. His son, Joey DeMio, spent time in Chicago and in a suite on the hotel's third floor. Carmine also owned a Victorian cottage on the East Bluff and spent most of the season on the Island.

I went in the front entrance, took off my coat and hung it on a rack by the door.

"Good afternoon, sir," said the Jamaican woman behind the counter. The nameplate on her blue blazer read, "Lucille Wallace."

"Hello," I said. "Michael Russo. I have an appointment with Mr. DeMio."

Lucille Wallace picked up the phone. "Mr. Russo, sir." She hung up the receiver. "Right this way, Mr. Russo."

"I know the way," I said, pointing to a short hallway behind the counter, to the right. "I'll knock first."

"Very good, sir," she said.

"Come in," a voice said after I knocked. I went in.

DeMio's office was just as elegant as the last time I was here.

A large square room with huge windows on the back wall. Floor to ceiling bookcases filled the other walls and the hardwood floor was mostly covered by an Oriental rug in dark red, blue and green. A big, ornate mahogany desk sat in front of the windows, and two loveseats sat across from each other next to a fireplace on the sidewall.

It was as just as I remembered it last time except that Carmine sat behind the desk and Joey stood by the fireplace. Not so this time. Joey sat behind his father's desk and Carmine sat on the loveseat closest to the desk. The power structure had changed even if the room had not.

"Joey," I said.

"Have a seat, counselor," Joey DeMio said from behind the desk.

I walked over to Carmine on my right, and we shook hands. "Carmine," I said. Carmine was a big man, maybe six-three, in his seventies with dark skin and thin black hair combed back flat. He wore a gray sharkskin suit, single-breasted, a black silk shirt open at the collar.

I moved to the desk and put out my hand for Joey. He was in no hurry, but he reached out and we shook hands. Joey was about one eighty-five and five-ten. He was fifty or fifty-one and trim enough for a man who worked out regularly. His skin was olive and his thick black hair was combed back.

Joey gestured at his father and sat down. Carmine got off the couch and came to the desk. "Sit, Michael," he said. I did.

"Michael, my son runs our businesses now. He has my full confidence." Carmine sat down in the other chair, next to me, in front of the desk. "After this day, you talk with Joseph. I speak to you now because I owe you a favor for helping Joseph last year." Carmine looked at his son. Joey showed no reaction at all. He may as well have been staring at the wall.

"As you know, this is not my son's favor, it is mine. Joseph has no obligation to you, but I asked him to honor my pledge and hear your request today."

Joey always believed it was his obligation. He was too proud not to. Joey believed he owed me for getting him out of the murder charge. No matter what his father said.

"Joseph," Carmine said, and he got out of the chair and returned to his seat by the fireplace. On the sidelines.

"What can I do for you, counselor?" Joey said.

"I need information," I said. Joey nodded. I resisted the temptation to look Carmine's way.

"You heard about the shooting in Petoskey a few weeks back? Frank Marshall?" Joey nodded again.

"The cops have no leads, no suspects, nothing."

"I wouldn't expect anything different," Joey said. "Why do you?"

"Because Martin Fleener is a smart cop," I said.

"Your opinion," Joey said with a dismissive tone. "My experience says different." Would have loved to smack the jerk. For the helluva it. Resisted that temptation, too.

"I'm after the shooters," I said. "That's why I'm here."

"Get on with it, counselor," Joey said.

"Good reason to believe the order for the hit came from Chicago." Joey's eyes moved to his father. It was quick, but I caught it.

"Marshall worked in Chicago for years as an investigator."

"I know about that," Joey said.

"He often encountered people, shall we say, in your line of work. Marshall wasn't shot by a couple of bums out to roust somebody. It was a hit."

"This where I come in?" Joey said.

I nodded. "I want to know who ordered it and who the two shooters were. I'll take it from there."

"Chicago's a big city, counselor," Joey said.

"Got a name for you," I said.

"And that is?"

"Rick Morgan." Joey shot Carmine a fast look again. Caught this one, too. I was ready for it. Just in case.

"Know the name?" I asked.

Joey nodded. "What's the story?"

"Marshall got tangled up with Morgan about twenty years ago."

"Twenty years ago?" Joey said, shaking his head.

"This was personal. About getting even no matter how long it took. Did Morgan order the hit or not? Who did the shooting? That's all I want to know."

Joey sat quietly for a minute, leaning on the desk.

"I'll get you the information, counselor," Joey said, "to the extent that doing so does not conflict with our interests. Another thing, Russo. Keep the cops out of this. They think I'm involved, or my father, we get trouble. You want information, you do it my way. Agreed?"

"Will you tell me if a conflict exists," I said, "so I'll know I missed something?"

Joey smiled. "Smart guy, Russo." He nodded. "Yes, that I can do." He stood up and I stood, too. The meeting was over.

"My secretary will call you when I have something."

"Joey," I said, "thank you." I turned towards the fireplace. "Carmine. Thank you, too." He nodded. "Gentlemen," I said and left the office.

I got my coat off the rack by the front door, put it on and went outside. The air was chilly and dark gray clouds hung low over the harbor. The flag at the end of the Arnold dock moved hard from the west. I went back across the park the way I came. Rick Morgan may not be tied to the Marshall shooting, but his name certainly got a reaction out of DeMio. Wonder why.

14

AJ was on the bed with a pillow propped up behind her head reading the *New York Times* when I got back to the Cloghaun. She looked up.

"Glad you're back," she said. "I'm starved."

"Hello to you, too," I said. "Me, too."

AJ got off the bed and grabbed her coat. "Let's go, Russo."

We walked down Hoban, holding hands.

"We going to the 'VI?'" I said.

"Sure," AJ said, and squeezed my hand.

The Village Inn, recently Cawthorne's Village Inn, has been a year-round mainstay on Mackinac since the 1980s. The big room, with lots of wood and print wallpaper, was split with a half wall divider, restaurant on one side, bar on the other.

The bartender saw us walk in. "Hi," he said. "Anywhere you like." One booth and a four-top in the middle of the floor were busy with eaters. That was it except for three men sitting together at the bar.

We picked the first booth, hung up our coats and sat down.

"Want the TV on?" AJ said. Each booth had a small TV hung on the wall, table high.

I shook my head. "Only want to gaze into your eyes."

"Oh, shut up," she said.

"That's encouraging," I said. "Makes me feel all warm and fuzzy."

"Good evening," said our waitress. She put menus in front of us. Her nameplate read, "Elizabeth, 6 years." She was in her late twenties with a soft face, round eyes and short brown hair with highlights in front. She wore a black skirt, a few inches above the knee, and a white shirt, cotton, open at the neck.

"Would you care for a drink?"

AJ ordered a house Chardonnay. I had a Dewer's and rocks.

Elizabeth came back a few minutes later and put coasters and our drinks on the table.

AJ lifted her wine glass. "A toast to our mini-vacation," she said.

"I'll drink to that," I said and touched her glass.

Elizabeth returned and said, "Are you ready to order?"

"Club sandwich on wheat toast and fries, please," AJ said. I ordered the spaghetti and meatballs.

"Spaghetti on Mackinac?" AJ said.

"Couldn't resist," I said. "Besides, since when is a club sandwich native to Mackinac?"

AJ shrugged and raised her glass again. "Here's to Carmine getting something on Rick Morgan." I clinked her glass with mine. We each took a drink.

"It's Joey we should toast," I said.

"Really? Why?"

I told her.

"You think Carmine's all done?"

I shrugged. "Worry about that later," I said. "More interested in Morgan."

"Fill me in, will ya?" I did.

"The reaction to Morgan's name could mean anything."

"Uh-huh," I said. "Only thing I know for sure is that it got a reaction."

"I'm betting they know the guy," AJ said. "Carmine's gotta be about the same age. Both from Chicago, both Mafia. Joey warned you about, what was the line?"

"You mean when he said 'our interests?'"

AJ nodded. "Sounds like family business to me. Besides, the meeting ended pretty quickly after that."

"Yeah."

Elizabeth put down two plates of food and some rolls. "Enjoy," she said.

I dug in to my spaghetti.

"As good as you remember, darling?" I nodded and smiled.

AJ flattened her sandwich with the palm of her hand. "See if I can get this thing into my mouth."

"Mouth's big enough for lots of things, darling," I said.

She looked at me over the top of her sandwich held in the air with both hands. "Can you get through a day and not think about sex?"

"Not if I'm around you, my sweet . . ." I said, raising my hands in surrender.

"Didn't miss the cleavage on the blond over there," AJ said, nodding in the direction of the table near ours.

"Hard to miss," I said.

"True," she said. "Focus on your Marinara sauce, dear, and I'll make you forget her cleavage later."

"I'll drink to that," I said and did. "Want another glass?" AJ nodded.

"If DeMio finds out that Morgan ordered the attack on Frank," AJ said, "then what? Take it to Fleener?"

"What's the point," I said. "Let's say Morgan tells a couple of wiseguys in Chicago to hustle up to Northern Michigan to kill a guy. Where's the evidence?"

Elizabeth put down two fresh drinks. I drank some scotch.

"Fleener and Hendricks had their chance. It didn't work. I'll get them myself."

"Yes," AJ said, "you will."

We finished eating and Elizabeth gave us the check. I put down a credit card.

"Did you want to stare at the blond with cleavage on the way out?"

"Rather stare at you," I said.

"That can be arranged," she said and put her hand near the top of her neck. "I could unbutton the top buttons of my shirt. Right now."

"Ah, you're wearing a sweatshirt. What am I supposed to see?"

"Use your imagination."

"I am."

"Let's get out of here," she said. "I'll hop in the claw-foot tub when we get back to our room."

"Thought you took a bath already?"

AJ's eyes narrowed. "You can join me in the tub."

We left the "VI" and walked up the street holding hands.

15

The clock on the side table said six-thirty. I'd been awake for ten minutes or so. AJ was sleeping soundly. The covers were pulled up, so all I could see was some black hair on the top of her head. Rain fell in a steady pattern on the roof. It didn't sound hard.

I laid the covers back and eased out of bed, trying to be quiet.

"You gonna run?" a voice said from under the covers.

"Yeah. Go back to sleep."

"Is that rain?" the voice said.

"Uh-huh," I said. "Go back to sleep."

I dug through my bag and pulled out a Gore-Tex jacket and pants and a hat. I grabbed my shoes and took it all into the bathroom to get dressed.

I turned out the bathroom light and quietly opened the door. I rummaged through my bag again, this time looking for my watch.

AJ slept quietly.

I slipped out the door and down the stairs. It was quiet downstairs, but I smelled fresh coffee brewing in the dining room. I stretched my hamstrings on the front porch. The rain had not gone away, but it wasn't any harder either. I pulled my hat down so the visor would block some of the water, clicked my watch and took off for Cadotte. I didn't mind the rain as long as it didn't turn into a storm with lightning and heavy wind. The isolation of a good run checked stress and gave me room to think, to analyze, or brainstorm a problem. That certainly was the case today. I eased into my pace up the hill, passing Grand Hotel. I cut up behind the hotel and headed for the Annex.

So what am I to think about Joey DeMio taking over the family business? Not sure. Biggest change would be for the wiseguys in Chicago not me. Carmine and I learned to trust each other during the Cherokee Point murder investigation, but I never got along with Joey. He lived to threaten people from time to time, including me. He lived to be a tough guy. Joey resented me not because I proved him innocent of murder, but because he felt he owed me a service for doing it.

The trees in the Annex blocked out some of the rain. I passed the airport, crossed Garrison Road and went into the woods on Crooked Tree. The trees were so thick that it was hard to tell it was raining.

I tried to tell Joey that he owed me nothing. His father tried to tell him the same thing. Joey didn't believe either of us. Doing business with Joey would always be more difficult with the debt hanging over his head. Sooner or later, he'd figure out a way to relieve himself of the burden.

I passed Sugar Loaf, went down to Arch Rock, and headed back in front of the cottages on the East Bluff. I went by DeMio's house, a Shingles Style it was called, covered in siding stained brown and white. The new cedar shake roof had begun to darken in the weather extremes of the Island. No sign of life, but it was early. I took the stairs in the woods at the top of the East Bluff, came out behind the Marquette Park Hotel, and made my way through the wet grass to Main Street.

I went up Fort Street at Doud's and ran down Market. I pulled up short of the Cloghaun, clicked my watch off, and walked the last hundred feet or so. About the only thing I knew for sure was that Joey was the man. What role would Carmine play? Didn't know.

I took my wet shoes off on the front porch and went upstairs for a shower. A few guests sat at tables in the dining room, talking softly and drinking coffee. I didn't see AJ, and she wasn't in the room when I got there.

I filled a glass with water and drank most of it. I got out of my clothes and jumped in the shower.

I'd just finished dressing when AJ came through the door with two cups of coffee.

"Here," she said, handing me one of the cups.

"Thanks," I said. "You're wet." AJ wore a yellow rain slicker that glistened with beads of water. "Where've you been?"

"I needed fresh air," she said. "I wasn't gonna melt." She took off her coat and sat on the unmade bed. "I walked down to the water then took the boardwalk to the school."

The Mackinac Island Public School was a one-floor brick building with big windows and a full-sized gym built into the hillside. It sat on the water, just west of downtown. Students got to school using their feet, bikes, or in the winter, snowmobiles.

"Hard to imagine what it would be like," AJ said and drank some coffee.

"What would?" I said.

"Going to a school with fewer than a hundred students," she said. "I mean all of it, you know, K-12." She shook her head. "But I know how I can find out."

I waited. "Would you like me to ask or do you want to tell me?"

"You're no fun."

"Not what you said last night."

AJ smiled. "I love you," she said. "I hope you know that." She put her coffee down, got off the bed, put her arms around my neck and we kissed.

"I do know that," I said, "and I like that you remind me all the time."

AJ took her arms away.

"Aw, don't do that," I said.

"We can snuggle later, darling," she said, looking at her watch. "We gotta go. We're meeting Henri and Fran at the Biscuit."

"When did this happen?" I asked, taking a last drink of coffee.

"Saw Henri on the way back. He said Fran got back early and they'd meet us."

We grabbed our coats, our bags, left the Cloghaun and walked down Market Street. We took Astor Street and passed the Mackinac Sandal Company.

The Seabiscuit Café was on Main Street at the foot of Astor. Well over a hundred years ago it had been a bank, then retail shops before it became an intimate restaurant and bar with brick walls and hardwood floors. Its namesake was the famous racehorse of the 1930s and the place was filled with lots of horsey stuff.

"Over here," a voice said when we walked in. It was Henri from a booth in the front window. He sat with his back to the wall, facing the door. Always careful. Born and raised on the Island, Henri LaCroix was a businessman. He owned a building on Main Street, near the Shepler's dock, and an apartment building in Harrisonville, the Village it was called, in the middle of the Island. But he was more than that. LaCroix was the toughest man in a fight I'd ever seen. With or without the "Gen 4" Glock under his coat. With or without the Lex silencer that often went with it.

Sitting next to Henri was Fran Warren who waved. Warren was in her early fifties, about five-seven, very trim, with soft blond hair that was slowly and elegantly turning gray.

"This was a good idea," AJ said. "Get a chance to catch up before we catch a boat."

Two white mugs of seaming coffee arrived at the table. Our waiter, a man in his twenties, not so tall, with a round face and long dark hair, put them in front of AJ and me.

"How was your run, Michael?" Fran asked. "Saw you over by the park."

"Good," I said. "Like the hills. Always have." I drank some coffee.

"Not me," Henri said. "I ran the shore road this morning."

"Yeah," Fran said, "I lapped you three times."

"You were on a racing bike," he said.

"Details, details."

"How'd your meeting with Joey go?" Henri asked.

I laughed. "Does anything around here miss you?"

"No," Henri said with a sly smile.

"Caught that you said, 'Joey' and not 'Carmine,'" I said.

"Change of command."

"Think it's real this time?" I said.

Henri nodded. "Unless Joey fucks up. Carmine'll come down on him hard if he does."

"How will we know?" I said.

"I'll know," Henri said.

"Of course you will, Henri," AJ said and smiled.

We talked pleasantly and drank coffee. I'd known Fran Warren longer than Henri LaCroix, but I trusted both of them. They were two people comfortable with themselves. Their advice was always thoughtful and offered genuinely.

"Did Joey have any idea who shot Frank Marshall?" Fran said.

"Not that he said."

I told them about Chicago and Rick Morgan.

I glanced at each of them. "What do you think?"

Henri shrugged. "Get back to me after you hear from Joey."

I looked at Fran. "Ditto," she said.

"Not very helpful," I said.

"I bought the coffee," Fran said. "What more do you want?"

"Hey," AJ said, surprising all of us. "We gotta go or we'll miss the ferry."

We slid out of the booth. We put our coats on, said our good-byes, and left the Biscuit.

We weren't the last ones to climb aboard the ferry, but it was close.

"Damn," AJ said, as we sat down in the last row.

I looked at her. "What?"

"I forgot to ask Henri about going to school here."

16

Life doesn't get any better than this. Leaning back in my chair, feet on the desk, a mug of hot coffee, reading Maureen Dowd's latest takedown of people in power. Well a few paying clients would be nice.

"Morning, Michael," Sandy said, looking into my office as she took off her coat.

"Where you been?"

"Errands," she said. "See your messages?"

I shook my head.

"Maureen," I said, pointing to the *New York Times*.

"Could you put the paper down long enough to see that we might have a new client?"

"Really?" I dropped my feet to the floor, found the note and read it.

"He wants you to call back before he makes an appointment."

"I'll do that," I said. "Anything else or can I move on to Frank Bruni?"

"There is something else," she said. "Let me get some coffee first."

Sandy came back, sat down and put a mug on the desk.

"Two things," she said. "I talked with Ellen Paxton. The hospital sent Frank home first thing this morning."

"That is good to hear," I said. "After all those days in the hospital . . . wow. Good for him. Ellen, too."

"He needs to stay close to home while his energy comes back."

"I'll call," I said. "What else?"

"Pam Wiecek," Sandy said. "She's called several times. Wants to know if you've found her sister."

"What'd you tell her?"

PETER MARABELL

"Said we found her but hadn't bothered to call."

"You didn't."

"Of course not," Sandy said, "but I felt like it. Woman's a pest."

I drank some coffee. "Maybe so," I said, "but I got to get up to that bar in Mac City. See what I can find out about Laurie Wiecek and her boyfriend. Place used to be a crummy hamburger joint."

"Bernie's?"

"Un-huh."

"It's still a crummy hamburger joint," Sandy said, "but they got booze."

"You a regular?"

Sandy shook her head. "Got a couple of friends like the Horseburger," she said. "Meet them once in a while."

"Horseburger?"

"That's what they call it," she said, holding up her right hand as if taking an oath. "So help me. It's on the menu."

I finished my coffee. "Well, I need to run up there and see what I can find out."

Sandy got out of her chair. "Got work to do," she said. "I'm leaving early, boss, gonna run to Gaylord this afternoon before I go home."

"Okay."

I swiped the screen on my phone and tapped AJ's number. She answered on the first ring.

"Hello, my love," I said. "Been thinking about hamburgers this afternoon . . ."

"So you called me. How sweet."

I ignored her sarcasm. Must be feeling generous.

". . . and I thought we could meet at the Side Door for a burger after work. What d'ya think?"

"I think, okay," she said. "How about six?"

"See you then," I said, and clicked the phone.

The afternoon marched along pleasantly. Sandy had gone for the day. I polished off a Cobb salad from Twisted Olive Café while I finished the

Times and moved on to *Runner's World*. I was happily indulging my fantasy of training for the Chicago Marathon when the outside door opened.

"Hello?" A man's voice said. "Mr. Russo?"

I closed the magazine and hauled myself out the chair.

"Yes?" I said, going to the front room.

The voice belonged to a man, about five-nine, maybe thirty-five, and a little on the heavy side. His pale face was partially hidden behind thick brown eyeglass frames. His brown hair was combed smoothly on his head. I could see a paisley bow tie and white shirt under a non-descript dark gray raincoat, the kind with the flap that hid the buttons.

He smiled, half-heartedly and said, "Michael Russo, I presume?" and put out his hand.

"Yes," I said, and shook his hand.

"Sorry for not calling first," he said, "but I was down the street." He handed me a card. It read, "James Kellerman, Attorney at Law."

"What can I do for you," I looked at the card again, "Mr. Kellerman?"

"Just a few moments of your time," he said.

"Come in," I said and we went to my office. Kellerman took off his raincoat and put over the back of the client chair. He wore a brown tweed jacket and tan cord pants with green little ducks all over them.

"Your card says, 'Petoskey.' Thought I knew all the lawyers around here."

"I only have a few clients," he said, "some businesses, some individuals."

"Where's your office?" I asked.

"I work out of my house, actually," he said, "off Pickerel Lake Road." He gestured in the general direction of north of town.

"Well, Mr. Kellerman, how can I help you?" I leaned back in my chair and folded my arms across my chest.

He reached forward to take one of my cards from the small wood holder at the edge of the desk. "May I?" he said.

I nodded.

He looked at the card for more than a moment. Shouldn't take that much effort to read a business card.

"Says here you're an attorney."

"That's me," I said and smiled.

He put the card in his jacket pocket.

"Then why are you acting like a private eye?" He wasn't smiling. Had a feeling this would not go well.

"None of your business, Mr. Kellerman."

"Oh, come now, Mr. Russo," he said, "don't be defensive. It's just one professional asking another."

Defensive? Me?

"Okay," I said, "you're right." I leaned forward and put my elbows on the desk. "Truth be told, I need the cash," I said.

"What?"

"The extra cash. Got my eye on a really sharp Porsche Carrera in Detroit. It ain't cheap, believe me."

His eyes narrowed. "I'm serious, Mr. Russo."

"Me, too," I said, faking a boyish excitement. "It's red over black leather, twin-turbo, only three-thousand miles."

He glared at me and his words came out slowly.

"You're messing with matters you know nothing about. You should direct your attention elsewhere, sir."

"Think I oughta stick with BMW, is that it?"

"All right, Mr. Russo, play your little games. Let me be clear. It would be healthier for you to mind your own business. Important people, people you don't know, are annoyed with you playing a private dick. Stay out of matters that don't concern you."

"You here on your own, or do you speak for a client?"

"Both," he said. "I speak for myself so my client won't have to, shall we say, insist."

"I don't enjoy being threatened, Mr. Kellerman."

"Then do as my client wishes, sir."

"Who's your client?"

He smiled. "You know better than that, Mr. Russo."

Enough of this. I stood up. "Friend of mine gets gunned down, it concerns me. Now get out."

Kellerman stood up. He put his coat on, slowly. "You'll hear from us again, Mr. Russo."

Us?

"We won't be so nice next time. Think about it."

He turned and left. I heard the door close and his shoes on the stairs.

I sat back down, put my feet on the corner of the desk and my hands behind my head. "Must've pissed somebody off," I said to an empty office.

17

finished making notes for two clients, one a divorce, the other a will on its way to Probate. I turned out the lamp on my desk and the overheads in the outer office and went to meet AJ.

I crossed the parking lot and turned up Bay before I realized I was on the lookout. For what? I'm not sure. A car? A guy jumping out of a doorway? I hadn't thought about Kellerman's visit the rest of the afternoon, but it obviously registered. Don't get threatened very often.

I punched the door locks and the inside lights came on. Nobody hiding behind the driver's seat. I put my brief bag in the back and got in. Traffic was light, so I went up U.S. 31 through Bay View and turned in at the Side Door Saloon.

AJ was standing at the bar, talking with reporter Lenny Stern. He could have been wearing the same tired black suit he wore the other day. But his tie was loose at the neck. Must be Lenny's concession to the casual workplace.

AJ saw me and waved. She wore gray wool slacks, a navy cardigan sweater over a navy and white wide striped shirt.

"Hello, Lenny," I said, as I leaned in and kissed AJ.

"Michael," he said, "good to see you, again." He reached out and we shook hands.

"You two figure out the future of journalism?"

"I wish," AJ said, and both of them laughed.

"Want to grab a sandwich with us?" I asked.

Lenny shook his head. "Going home," he said. "But I got some information might interest you."

"Okay."

"Tom Marshall," he said. "Frank's brother? I found him."

I nodded. "I'm listening."

"He's lives in Sedona."

"Arizona?"

"You know another Sedona?" he said, shaking his head.

"Sorry," I said. "Go ahead."

"He's got a small house in the old section of town, just off the main drag."

"Lenny," I said. "Did you just happen on news about Tom, or'd you go looking?"

Lenny got this sheepish grin on his face. AJ laughed and said, "This is what he does, Michael. He gets a name or a place or something and that's it. He's tenacious, to say the least. He does this all the time."

"Look, Michael," Lenny said. "I knew some people used to be at the University of Chicago. Couple of 'em still there. I asked around."

"They remember Tom?"

"One guy did, sort of, but Tom Marshall is on the University mailing list." Lenny shrugged. "The rest was easy." He looked at his empty beer glass and pushed it away.

"He works at a small tourist place north of town," he said. "The 'Bunny Bear Inn'" or 'The Running Rabbit Resort.' Some silly name like that."

"He a teacher?"

"Of sorts," Lenny said. "He teaches Yoga."

"Yoga?" I said. "A History professor?"

Lenny shrugged and looked at his empty beer glass again. "Woman he lives with owns a studio in town. Marshall teaches the satellite class at the bunny place."

"He has to be in his sixties," AJ said.

"That's about right," I said. "Frank's a few years older."

"The Yoga woman's early forties," Lenny said. "Good looking if her website photos are for real."

"You really dug around, didn't you?" I said.

He shrugged. "Better to know more than know less," Lenny said. "Thought it might help you some way."

I nodded. "Thanks," I said. "It might."

Lenny glanced one last time at his glass and got up. "Time to go," he said.

AJ and I said good-bye to Lenny Stern and found a two-top on the far wall.

"You have a long day?"

AJ nodded.

"Not bad," she said. "Difficult, but not bad."

Our waitress appeared, took our drink order and left.

"Same old stuff or something new?"

"Internet edition's okay, so far," AJ said. "I've been talking to Maury about a blog. You know, two or three of us would contribute every day. Maybe several times a day. Local news and sports or emergencies."

"You mean, 'breaking news?'"

"God, I hope not. Talk about an overworked phrase," she said. "Every time that pops up I want to change the channel."

"But you don't."

"Of course I don't," AJ said. "Might miss something."

The waitress put down a Chardonnay for AJ and a Dewer's and rocks for me. I took a drink. We ordered burgers, deluxe, one medium, one well.

"Still no fries?" I asked the waitress.

She shook her head slowly, no doubt tired of having to answer "why not" too many times. So I didn't ask.

"Chips'll be fine," I said and she went away.

"You got any 'breaking news' for me?" AJ asked.

"There's a fire in your eyes."

"Wishful thinking, darling," she said. "Two proposals need work tonight and I got an early meeting."

"That mean I'm sleeping alone?"

The waitress put two burgers on the table, and I ordered another round of drinks.

AJ raised her wine glass. "How about tomorrow night. I'll stop on the way home and get a small pork loin. You can cook."

"The rosemary and sage rub?"

AJ clinked my glass. "That's the one," she said. "After dinner, some serious body rubbing." She smiled.

"Deal," I said. I took a large bite out of my burger and ate a potato chip.

"I'm gonna run up to Mac City for a drink after work tomorrow. Want to join me?"

AJ finished chewing a mouthful of burger. "Can't we go to City Park Grill or come back here?"

I shook my head. "Have to check out Bernie's. See what I can find out about Pam Wiecek's sister."

"That the dump on Nicolet?"

"Uh-huh."

"No, thanks," she said. "I'll have wine at home." AJ ate a potato chip. "You'll recognize me when you get back. I'll be the dame with very few clothes on. Even less underwear." She smiled again.

"You are fun, my love," I said. "Think we'll make it 'till after dinner?"

"How long's the roast take?"

"About an hour, give or take."

"What a coincidence."

We leaned across the table and she kissed me.

The waitress cleared the leftovers and brought the check. I paid cash and left a tip.

We walked outside to the parking lot holding hands. "You going to tell Frank about his brother?"

"Yeah," I said. "Let him decide if he wants to do anything with the information."

"That's probably best," AJ said. "Will it help you at all?"

"Haven't got a clue," I said.

"Not many clues hanging around, are there?"

"No."

AJ beeped the door locks of her SUV.

"Don't you think it's time to trade that truck for a car?"

"You've been asking me that since I got it," she said. "It's not a truck and the answer's still no."

I laughed. "Well then, give me a hug."

We held each other for a long minute and kissed good night.

"Sleep tight," I said. "I'll talk to you tomorrow."

AJ drove off and I got into my BMW. A real car.

I pushed the start button and the twin-turbo V-6 snarled to life. The dashboard lights glowed a menacing orange. I sat for a moment with my hands on the small, thick sports steering wheel and smiled. But it wasn't Bavarian engineering on my mind this time.

I made a conscious decision not to mention my unexpected visitor to AJ. It's hard to forget being threatened, but I didn't want to tell her just yet.

I pulled out on U.S. 31 and headed home through Bay View. Something didn't add up. Don Hendricks and Martin Fleener were annoyed that I started tracking the shooters, but I expected that.

Only other thing I did was talk to Joey DeMio.

Would DeMio threaten me? Yes. Would he send a hambone like Kellerman to do it? Not likely. DeMio'd send the family muscle, Santino Cicci and Gino Rosato. He'd done that before. I should ask Joey.

Plenty of time for that after I check out Mr. James Kellerman.

18

Sandy and I spent the better part of the day tracking James Kellerman. Phone calls, internet searches, even the Chamber of Commerce.

Sandy sat down with a mug of coffee.

"Want some?" she said.

"Enough caffeine for one day," I said. I cleared a spot on the desk for my elbows and leaned forward. "Well?"

"Well, not much," Sandy said, "and that's being optimistic."

"Let's go over it one last time." I looked at my watch. "Then I need to get to Mackinaw City."

"Bernie's?"

I nodded.

"You gonna have a Horseburger?"

"Gonna ask questions about the missing Wiecek sister. Think about Trigger later."

"Cute."

"Thank you," I said, faking a smile. "Kellerman?"

Sandy nodded and went to a yellow pad in her lap.

"Nothing. Nothing helpful, anyway." She flipped through a few pages. "Calls, the internet, and the phone book, both electronic and dead trees versions, I got nothing substantial."

Sandy drank some coffee.

"Checked the ABA. Membership and group memberships, just in case. The renewal year started on September first, so I checked last year, too. Nothing. Checked the State Bar and came up empty. Even checked out Legal Services up here. Gaylord and Sault Ste. Marie."

"Think he's volunteered?"

"Hey," she said, "you never know. But I drew a blank there, too." Sandy took a deep breath and let it out slowly. "I did find one small lead. Very small."

"Yes?"

"A James Kellerman lives in Grosse Point Park."

"Address or phone?" I said.

Sandy shook her head. "P.O. box. But, the same Kellerman owns a few properties in Emmet County. South of town on the Charlevoix Road, on Pickerel Lake Road and just outside of Levering."

"He said he worked from a house on Pickerel Lake Road."

I stretched my arms over my head to get the kinks out. "Wonder if Bill Stapleton could help?" Bill Stapleton was a partner at Pennington, Gray and Stapleton, a Birmingham law firm. We met in law school and I worked at Pennington, Gray for two years after graduation. We shared a love for the law and fast cars.

"Way ahead of you," Sandy said. "He's out of the office until tomorrow. Left a voicemail that you wanted to talk hot cars."

"You lied to a lawyer?"

"Figured he'd call quicker to talk cars."

I laughed. "Are we that predictable?"

The look on her face said I'd just asked a very dumb question.

Sandy flipped the pages of her pad and picked up her mug.

"That's enough, Michael," she said. "Time for me to go home. Sip a Maker's Mark. Cook some dinner." She stood up. "One more thing."

"Yeah?"

"Change your clothes. Dress down before you go to Bernie's."

I looked down, at me. "Khakis and a crewneck sweater? This is down."

"Dress differently then. Bernie's is about as local as a place can be."

"All I'm gonna do is ask a few questions." I said. "Don't need a wardrobe change for that. How much trouble can I get in?"

"Suit yourself," she said. "Pun intended."

I laughed. "Got me on that one," I said.

"Hop in that hot car of yours and race up to Bernie's."

"Okay," I said. "Go home. I'll see you in the morning."

19

The sun glowed low in the sky as I crossed the parking lot behind my building. The lights at the Twisted Olive Café looked mighty inviting. AJ and I could be eating a quiet, intimate dinner looking at the Bay. Instead, Bernie's. I went to my car, put my coat and bag on the rear seat and got going.

Most of the commuter traffic was ahead of me. Very little congestion in Alanson or Pellston. Forty-five minutes later, I turned off Nicolet Street at Bernie's, a one-story, red brick building with plenty of windows on the two sides facing the parking lot. All the windows but one by the door had long since been covered over from the inside. A three-foot wide strip of dirt lined the building's walls. Long ago it might have been landscaped with shrubs and a few flowers. Now it collected twigs, dead cigarettes and scraps of paper.

A big red neon sign jutted out over the door. In large script, it read, "BA." The "R" was dark. I'd bet a beer no one noticed. Or cared.

I parked off to the side, away from the four pickup trucks jammed close to the door. Anyone drive a car?

I pushed through the door into a large basement of a room. The bar, on the right, stretched from the front wall back to an opening that was likely the kitchen. Stools with chrome legs and red plastic seats formed an uneven line in front of the bar. A long mirror hung on the wall behind the bar. In various places it said, "Budweiser," or "Molson," or "Pabst Blue Ribbon." No mention of Newcastle Brown Ale. Tables for two and four, the kind that customers could shove around to fit more people, were scattered over the rest of the floor.

In the back corner, next to the restrooms, sat three pinball machines. Only one flashed its lights and no one played.

Ambient lighting at Bernie's pretty much consisted of the bright white light that shot out of the kitchen.

I hung my coat on a hook at the door. Two guys sat at one end of the bar and three others sat a small table in the middle of the room. Add the bartender, and six men watched every step I took to the far end of the bar where I climbed onto a stool.

The bartender, a big guy with sloping round shoulders and a thick middle, wiped his hands on a towel and ambled my way. He wore a heavy denim shirt, sleeves rolled up to the elbow, and a dirty white apron tied a few inches above his waist.

He stopped in front of me, put both hands on his side of the bar, and said, "What can I get you?"

"A beer," I said. "What d'ya got?"

"Everything," he said, bored.

"A Bell's Oberon."

"Don't have it," he said.

"Goose Island?"

"Don't have it."

"What do you have, then," I said.

"Bud, Bud Light, Miller, Miller Light . . ."

"A Budweiser," I said. "No glass."

He turned to his left, raised a dented stainless lid and pulled out a bottle of Bud. In one fluid motion, he turned back to the bar, his arm already moving downward and struck the opener. The tin cap bounced to the floor behind the bar. He put the bottle in front of me.

"See a menu?"

He leaned over, pulled a menu from under the bar, and dropped it in front of me. He walked away. I looked at a stained, wrinkled sheet of paper. Not sure I wanted to touch it, but I'm a tough guy.

Didn't take long to find it. "Bernie's Famous Horseburger." It came with most of the trimmings. American cheese was an extra cost option.

I sipped my beer and surveyed the room. Didn't look any worse from my seat than it did from the door. At least no one paid me any attention now. Except the bartender who came back my way.

"What can I get ya?" he said.

"Think I'll stick with the beer."

He nodded and took the menu. I put a five on the bar.

"Got a question for you," I said.

"Yeah?" he said, still bored.

"Looking for Shane Malone."

"Who are you?"

"Name's Russo," I said. "You Malone?"

"Maybe," he said.

Maybe? This guy was starting to annoy me. Maybe?

"Want to talk to the manager," I said. "Are you Shane Malone?"

He nodded. "Want d'ya want?"

"Looking for a woman used to work here," I said.

Malone stretched out his arms and leaned on the bar. "You don't look like a cop," he said.

"Private," I said. I put a picture down for Malone to see. "Her name's Laurie Wiecek."

Malone straightened up. "That broad," he said. "All tits and stringy hair." He wasn't bored anymore. His face was suspicious, maybe angry. "What's her to you?"

"She's missing," I said. "Sister can't find her, so I'm looking."

"You get paid to do this?"

Malone was annoying, but I ignored his question. "When's the last time you saw her?"

"Easy life," he said. "Get money to ask questions. How much you paid?"

"None of your business, Shane," I said. "When did you last see her? She ran off with her boyfriend. Guy named Eddie."

"Eddie Garner," he said, shaking his head. "Catch that prick, I beat the shit outta him."

"Laurie Wiecek?" I said.

"Her, too," he said. "Beat her, too." It was anger now, on his face and in his voice. "You know 'bout those two?"

The guys at the other end of the bar watched us.

"Why don't you tell me, Shane," I said.

"Took the weekend's till when they ran off. Almost three large." He pointed a beefy finger at me. "You gonna find my money?" he said. "You from downstate?"

"Petoskey," I said. "You call the cops?"

"I take care of Garner my way. Don't need cops."

"You haven't found either one of them doing it your way, Shane."

He glared at me.

"You know where Garner and Wiecek ran to?"

"You ask a lot of question, buddy," he said. "You know that?" The table of men was looking our way, too. Probably wanted to know what Malone was going to do. Or maybe they knew and were waiting for it.

"Look, Shane," I said. "I can help you."

"How's that?"

"I find the woman, you get Garner." It was obvious he hadn't thought of that. "Where would they go? Friends? Family?"

"You ask too many questions," Malone said. Loud enough that the other men didn't have to strain to hear.

"You said that already, now where would they go?"

Malone grabbed my half full bottle of Bud and made one pass over the bar with a dirty white towel. He picked up my five and tossed at me. "Get outta here," he said. "Your money's no good. Go on."

I slid off the stool. The audience wondered if I was about to do something.

"Ever heard of Alan Ladd, Shane?" I asked.

"Out," he said. "And stay out. We know how to take care of people like you."

"Keep the five," I said. "Paint the place."

Malone put his fist in the air. "Take care of you now, you don't move it."

I walked towards the door.

"Hey," I said.

Malone glared at me.

"That mean I can't come back, Shane?"

"Move it."

I put on my coat and went out into the night air. It felt cold, like late fall into winter. I thought I saw a few flurries in the soft glow of the streetlights on Nicolet.

I beeped the door locks.

"You," a man's voice said behind me.

I turned to see two men move out of the shadow of Bernie's into the light of the parking lot. Both were young, in their twenties and over six-feet tall. They wore baggy jeans and thick plaid wool shirts. Their hands were not in their pockets. They came towards me side-by-side.

"Wanna talk to you, shithead."

Shithead? Guess I didn't get out of Bernie's fast enough for Malone.

I leaned against the car and folded my arms, like I was amused.

"For crissake," I said, "didn't see you guys inside. Tell Malone I won't bother him again."

The two men looked at each other. Guy on the left said, "Don't know any Malone. Been tailin' you." He stretched out his arm and pointed at me. "We came for you, Russo."

He knew my name but not Malone's. Think fast. This isn't karate class. Get out in the open. I slid sideways, slowly, down the length of the BMW so nothing was behind me but air.

The men moved with me but still didn't move apart. Amateurs. Pros would separate to make a triangle. Make it harder for me to fight.

"Time to mind your own business," said the other one. His head was shaved, his face puffy with too much beer.

They moved closer and I spread my feet apart but didn't back up.

"Ya got asked nice," said Mr. shaved head. "But you didn't listen." He wagged his finger this time. "One more chance or we beat the shit out of you."

The man on the left, taller, with a hard face said, "Don't stick your nose where it don't belong."

I didn't say anything.

"People in Chicago don't like you asking questions. Got that? Stop or they might shoot you, too." This guy pointed a finger at me, too. "Say you're gonna stop or we beat you into the ground."

"Didn't your mother tell you it was rude to point?" Maybe it'd buy me a second or two.

"Oh," Mr. shaved head said, "a smart ass."

I went at him first. My left arm shot up from my side, fingers back, palm out. It moved in an arc, fully extended when it caught him below the chin and snapped his head back.

"Ahh," he yelled, stumbling back a step. He landed on the ground, grabbing his throat.

I turned to the other man just in time to see his left fist swing my way, like a big, grand gesture. I ducked down, not to the side, just like I learned in class and he missed. But his puffy face belied his speed. His right fist caught me on the temple, at my left eye. I staggered backwards as his left fist caught the other side of my head, above the right ear. I saw his right fist in a wide arc coming . . .

20

What's that sound? I can't make that out. That sound. What is it?

I heard a voice, too. My voice? Somebody else's voice?

"It's the electronic monitor, Russo," the other voice said. My right eye opened more easily than my left eye. Didn't hurt as much either. Everything's kinda blurry.

The other voice belonged to Martin Fleener.

"Marty?" I said, softly. I tried to move but everything hurt. "Where am I?"

"Petoskey. Emergency room."

A face moved between Fleener and me.

"Mr. Russo?" It was a woman in a long white coat. Must be a doctor. Her name was stitched above the left breast pocket, but I couldn't read it. "You'll be a bit groggy for a while. We gave you a sedative when you got here."

"What happened?" I said.

"Well, the Captain, here, can tell you that," the doctor said. We were in a small room with a bed, two industrial chairs and a wall full of medical supplies. "You'll be okay, but you got worked over pretty good. Banged up rib cage, but nothing broken. A couple of bruises around your groin. Probably got kicked. No damage there, either. Your head, especially that left eye, will hurt a lot. We gave you five stitches to close the cut. And you'll have a world-class shiner."

"Thank you," I said.

"You're welcome," she said. "Gotta go. It's a busy night."

Fleener stood next to the bed. "You don't look so good," he said.

"Feel worse," I said. "How'd I get here?"

"Tell me about the bar first."

I told him about my night at Bernie's.

"Recognize them?"

I tried to shake my head, but it hurt. "No," I said instead. "Know 'em if I see 'em again."

"Look at pictures later?"

"Uh-huh," I said.

"You want to file a complaint?"

"I do," I said, "but how'd I get here?"

"Citizen found you in the parking lot. Thought you'd passed out. Called the cops. They took one look you at you and called it in. You got a fast ride down 31."

"How'd you get here?" I said.

"Petoskey officer recognized you when they brought you in. Knew we were friends."

The door opened and in walked AJ. She came right to me, leaned over and kissed my forehead. "Hi, sweetheart." She picked up my hand and kissed it, too. She looked at Marty and nodded. "Didn't think anything of it when you were late," she said.

"How'd you get here?"

"Marty called me. Came quick as I could." AJ took off her French blue parka. She wore a dull gray, paint stained sweatshirt and matching pants. Her stick-around-home outfit. She looked wonderful.

"Glad you're here," I said and squeezed her hand.

The door moved and in came Henri LaCroix. He went to the end of the bed.

"Michael," he said. "You all right?"

"Roughed up and sore, but I'll be okay."

Henri glanced to his right. "AJ," he said. "Captain."

Fleener went and stood face-to-face with Henri.

"You carrying?"

Henri nodded.

"Suppose you got a permit."

Henri nodded.

"You oughta get out of here until we're done," Fleener said.

Henri shook his head.

"It wasn't a request."

"Marty," AJ said. "I called Henri. I want him here. I want him with Michael until you catch these two."

Fleener stayed next to Henri. "Keep out of trouble, LaCroix," Fleener said. "You hear me?"

"Do the best I can, Captain. Don't plan to shoot anybody. Unless I have to."

"Make sure you don't have to," Fleener said.

Henri shrugged.

"You know who did this?" AJ said.

I tried shaking my head again. Didn't hurt quite as much, but I added, "No."

"Think they were the guys shot Frank Marshall?" Fleener said.

"Don't know," I said. I slowly pushed myself up on the pillows. Not easy to do.

"Pretty odd coincidence," Fleener said. "You poke around Marshall's shooting, talk to Joey DeMio. You get beat up."

"Looking at something else last night," I said.

"What would that be?" Fleener said.

I told him just enough about the missing Wiecek sister. "Well, we'll see," he said.

"But I'm not too worried about these guys," I said to all of them. Not a good comment. Henri stared at the wall, but otherwise didn't react. Fleener shook his head and ran the fingers of his right hand through his hair.

And AJ?

"Are you out of your mind?" she said. "Look at you. You're in the emergency room, for crissake." She turned to Henri. "Talk some sense to him, will ya?"

"Do what you need to do, Michael," Henri said. "I'll be around for a while."

"That's not what I meant, Henri," AJ said.

"Will you two cut it out?" I said, as loud as I could which wasn't very loud. They stopped. "Good. Would someone tell me where my car is?"

"Your car?" AJ said. "Are you . . ." She stopped mid-sentence. "Is that all you can think about? Your goddamn car?"

"I just want to know where it is," I said.

"Home," Fleener said. "Had one of the officers get it. It's at your apartment."

"Thanks, Marty."

"You're welcome," he said. "I know how you are. Didn't want to waste my time talking you out of getting it yourself."

"I need a drink," AJ said.

Fleener came over to the bed. "Gotta go," he said. "Come to the office tomorrow. We'll get your statement, look at some pictures. Okay?"

"Afternoon all right?" I said. "I'll call first."

"Sure." He said goodnight to AJ, nodded at Henri, and left.

AJ sat on the side of the bed and Henri pulled up one of the chairs.

"You leave anything out?" Henri said.

"Maybe a little," I said.

"Do I really want to hear this?" AJ said.

"You want to go home?" I said.

"Not going anywhere without you," she said.

"You were a little vague with Fleener," Henri said.

"Think he noticed?"

"Of course he noticed," Henri said. "He'll bring it up later."

"Were the guys last night the shooters, or not?" AJ said.

I shook my head. It hurt less. Progress. "No," I said, emphatically.

"You sound pretty sure," AJ said.

"I am. The guys last night were kids. Barely out of high school. They were big. Probably get money to scare people, but they're not shooters. They didn't know how to fight. No, these two were amateurs."

"Did a pretty good job on you, Russo," Henri said.

"Two against one."

"Yeah, yeah," he said.

"I'll get better at karate," I said. "Not as good as you, but better."

"Nobody's as good as me," Henri said. "But you better learn soon. We now got four bad guys to hunt down."

"We?"

Henri nodded. "Don't you want me to tag along?"

"Well, if he doesn't, I do," AJ said. "No arguments either, Michael. You hear?"

"Don't you have anything better to do, Henri?" I said.

"Nah. Collected the rents. Repairs're done."

The doctor returned to the room. She carried a clipboard.

"Mr. Russo," she said. "The report's good. No concussion. If your head's clear enough, go home." She looked at AJ and Henri. "Can one of you drive him home?"

"I can't drive?"

"Tomorrow, yes. Tonight, no," she said.

"We'll take good care of him," AJ said.

"Then I'll be on my way," the doctor said.

I thanked her and she left.

"I'm taking you to my house," AJ said. "Put you in the guestroom for the night." AJ slipped off the bed and picked up her coat.

"One more thing," I said.

AJ stopped. I looked at both of them.

"The two guys last night weren't the shooters, but they're part of it."

"How so?" Henri said.

"Couple of things," I said. "One guy said 'Chicago people.' That's how he said it, 'Chicago people,' wanted me to stop nosing around."

"So it wasn't a coincidence," AJ said.

I shook my head. Didn't hurt much at all.

"It had nothing to do with the missing woman then," AJ said.

I shook my head again. Much better.

"So what we got," Henri said, "is four bad guys in our neighborhood. An old mobster in Chicago. James Kellerman, Esquire, hanging around Petoskey. Not to mention Mackinac Island's favorite Mafia don."

"Looks that way," I said.

"Think they're all connected?" AJ said.

"I do," I said.

"How?"

"Haven't got a clue."

"Sure you do," Henri said. "You said it. Just now."

"I did?"

Henri nodded. "The guys who beat you up warned you off the Marshall shooting, talked about Chicago people. Right?"

"Yeah."

"Kellerman warned you, too. You pissed him off because you wouldn't listen and you got beat up."

"Kellerman?" I said.

"Only one linked to the others."

"So far," I said. "Don't know about Chicago yet. Haven't heard from DeMio."

"It's a place to start."

"Kellerman," I said.

Henri took a deep breath and let it out slowly. "Things starting to get ugly."

21

"**M**ichael, wake up."

"Guess I fell asleep."

"You closed your eyes as soon as we got you into the car."

Henri opened the passenger door on AJ's SUV and unbuckled my seatbelt.

"Think you can walk okay?" he said.

"Yeah," I said. "Not that woozy."

I swung both legs to the ground and used the door pillars to pull myself up. Henri stepped back. His Gen-4 Glock was in his right hand, down at his side.

"Think you're gonna need that to get me in the house?"

"I hope so," he said. "AJ, go ahead of us. Stay inside just in case."

AJ nodded and opened the back door, the one that led into the kitchen. Henri stayed close, between me and the street, until we got inside. I sat in a chair at the kitchen table.

"Do you want to stay here tonight, Henri?" AJ said.

"Don't need to," he said. "Teenage goons aren't gonna rush the house. The pros won't either. They'll plan a run at Michael, if they try it at all."

"Where you staying?" I said.

"The Perry," Henri said, smiling. "Always like it there." His gun was still at his side. "What time you want me here in the morning?"

"Think that's necessary?"

"Yes," he said. "In case somebody tries to follow you again."

"Michael," AJ said, sounding annoyed. Or exasperated. "I think it's necessary."

I nodded. "How about eight?" I said. "My apartment then to the office."

"In the morning then," Henri said and left the house.

"Come on, Michael," AJ said. "Let's get you to bed."

"I need a shower first," I said. "Too messed up to be comfortable."

"Okay," AJ said, "but I want you in a bathtub not standing in the shower."

"Only take a bath when we fool around," I said. "You wanna fool around?"

"Of course, I do, darling," AJ said. "Maybe tomorrow."

"Okay," I said. "Kinda sore right now."

"Upstairs we go," AJ said.

Thirty minutes later, I was as clean as a bath would get me and tucked safely under the covers in the guestroom. AJ sat on the side of the bed. She put a hand on my cheek.

"I'm more scared now than at the hospital," she said. "Didn't have time to think about it. Now I do and I'm scared."

"I'll be all right, sweetheart," I said. "Don't worry."

"I have a license to worry about you, Russo, because I love you." She picked up my left hand and kissed it. "I just have to worry about you in a different way," she said. "Gotta figure that out."

AJ leaned down and kissed me on the mouth. I returned the affection as best I could.

"I'll get you up for coffee before Henri gets here," she said.

"Any time after seven," I said. "Be nice to sit quietly, the two of us, for a little bit."

"That would be nice," AJ said. "Especially right now."

She got off the bed. I think she said goodnight on her way out. Not sure.

I pushed the button on my iPhone. It was 7:45. We sat at the kitchen table and drank coffee. We didn't talk much, but we held hands most of the time. I carefully touched the stitches. I'd developed quite a black eye overnight.

"What've you got going today?" AJ said.

"Not much. Catch up on a couple of files before I meet Fleener to look at mug shots," I said. "I hope I don't frighten Sandy when she sees my face."

"I talked with her last night."

"Last night?"

"Uh-huh," AJ said. "Called her after you went to sleep. I told her what happened."

"She okay?"

"Well, as okay as you can be when your boss got beat up."

"Thanks," I said.

There was a soft knock at the back door. It was Henri. AJ unlocked the door and he came in.

"Coffee?" she said.

Henri looked at me. "We got time?"

I nodded and Henri poured a mug of coffee and sat down.

"I hung around a while last night," he said. "See if anything developed." He shrugged. "Nothing did. After an hour, I went to the Perry."

"Were you in the backyard?" AJ said.

"Sort of," he said. "I parked over on Clinton," Henri pointed over his right shoulder. "Snuck behind the houses. Settled down in the trees. Pretty dull."

"That's a good thing," AJ said.

"Maybe, but I'd like to get this over with," Henri said. "Be ready when they come for us."

"Think they'll come?" I said.

He nodded. "It's a matter of who comes first, the pros or the amateurs."

"It'll be the kids," I said.

"What I think," Henri said.

"Why them?" AJ said.

"They're locals and they're here," Henri said. "They won't be patient. Don't know how."

"The pros might be here or gone," I said. "If they're still here, they will be patient. They'll wait for the right time because they're pros."

"That's not very reassuring," AJ said.

"Actually it is," Henri said. "Makes them more predictable. They'll only take a run at Michael if conditions are right. We're pros, too. We recognize a good set-up when we see one."

I looked at my watch. "Come on," I said. "Time to go."

Henri rinsed his mug out and put it in the sink. I did the same.

"Don't suppose I could walk home?"

"Another time," Henri said.

"It's only four blocks."

"You're pretty sore, Michael," AJ said.

I shrugged. "Okay. But I'm gonna take a real shower at my place." I glanced at AJ who was shaking her head.

"Stay in the car, Henri, or come in and make more coffee. Your choice."

"Get you safely to your apartment first," he said. "Then I'll wait and see what happens."

22

Sandy put a plate on the desk. It was filled with rolls, donuts and Danish from Johan's Bakery.

"I made the run," she said. "Not to mention making the coffee. I get first choice."

"Okay with me."

"Me, too," Henri said. "Bet you take the cinnamon sugar donuts."

Sandy smiled and put both of them on a napkin.

I reached for a raspberry Danish and Henri took a glazed donut. We drank coffee and enjoyed the carbohydrates for a few minutes.

Sandy shook her head.

"What?" I said.

"You really look awful," she said.

"Thanks a lot."

"You know what I mean. You look like a guy who got beat up."

"I am a guy who got beat up."

She turned to Henri. "Think you can keep this from happening again?"

Henri nodded. "Of course."

"How?" Sandy said.

"Could always shoot 'em," he said. "One at a time, same time." He shrugged.

"That gets my vote," Sandy said.

"Would the Lone Ranger and Billy the Kid wait long enough we could ask 'em questions?"

"Such as?" Sandy said.

"Who hired them, for one," I said, "if it's the local guys who show up first."

"What if the pros show up first?" Sandy said.

"The pros would be a problem."

Sandy shook her head. "Not sure I understand."

"What Michael means," Henri said, "the pros won't give us a chance to ask questions."

"Oh." Sandy hesitated, then, "Where does that leave us?"

I shrugged. "Kellerman's the only one linked to anyone else."

"We should go get Kellerman," Henri said.

I nodded. "Want to hear from DeMio," I said, "before we make a move like that."

"Shit," Sandy said. "Forgot." She came out of her chair almost dropping her mug trying to put it on the desk. "Got a message for you."

Sandy went out of the office and came back with a note.

"Sorry," she said. "With your ugly face and all, I forgot." She sat down. "Carlo Vollini called. Joey DeMio wants to see you tomorrow morning. His office. Eleven o'clock." She handed me the message.

"His office?" I said. "Guess that makes it official Joey's calling it his office."

"Guess so," Sandy said. "The new Don of Mackinac Island."

I looked over at Henri.

He smiled. "Need a good run on the hills of the Island," he said. "Want to join me?"

"Plenty of good hills right here in Petoskey," I said.

"Ain't the same," he said.

"Think you'll be in more danger on Mackinac?" Sandy said.

"Not sure," I said, "but I doubt it. No place to hide if they made a run at us. We know the geography better than they do."

"Our advantage," Henri said.

Sandy looked at her watch.

"What time you going to see Fleener?"

"In a little while," I said. "Couple of files I want to catch up on first."

Sandy picked up her mug. "You were talking about Kellerman," Sandy said, "when I remembered Vollini."

"Uh-huh," I said. "It's time to see where Kellerman hangs out. Don't have to go after him yet. I'll try to ID the guys who beat me up this afternoon. I see Joey tomorrow, so we're back to Kellerman."

"So you think he's connected to the guys last night. How about the shooters?" Sandy said.

"Last night, yes," I said. "Not sure about the shooters."

"I'll go over my notes again," Sandy said. "Might be something I missed."

"I'll make a few calls while you're with Fleener," Henri said.

"You don't want to go with me?"

Henri shook his head. "They're not too fond of me. Stay away unless I have no choice."

23

I sat at Martin Fleener's desk for better than two hours watching the slide show flash across his monitor. Didn't recognize one face.

We left his office and wound our way through the corridors of the County building to Don Hendricks' office, the epitome of quiet institutional. Muted colors everywhere, the walls, the furniture, the carpet. Hendricks sat behind a green metal desk with a brown Formica top. It was covered with papers, files and two corded telephones. Most annoying to Hendricks, as he would tell anyone who would listen, the windows didn't open.

Fleener took his usual chair, the walnut high back on the sidewall under the huge map of Emmet County. I sat in the chair in front of the desk.

Hendricks' heavy frame filled his chair. His jacket hung on the back of the door, his sleeves were pushed up his arms and his tie was loose at the collar.

"Marty tells me you're holding out on us, Russo."

I glanced at Fleener. I put my arms out, palms up.

"Don, come on, would I hold out on you guys?"

Hendricks nodded. "Yeah."

"Michael," Fleener said, "you know something about the Marshall shooting we oughta know?"

"Nothing solid enough to repeat," I said.

"Bullshit," Hendricks said. "Tell us what you know and let us decide."

This wasn't going well. Hendricks and Fleener are experienced at this sort of thing. Got to give them something.

"How 'bout I tell you what I'm clear on," I said, "and leave it at that? For now."

"How 'bout all of it?" Hendricks said.

I shook my head. "Only what I'm sure of," I said. "The rest later."

"Could throw your ass in jail," Hendricks said. "As a material witness."

"But you won't, Don," I said. "When I'm sure, okay?"

"Maybe," Hendricks said. "Let's have it."

"The guys last night?"

"Uh-huh."

"Not the shooters."

"You sure?"

I nodded.

"Because?" Hendricks said.

"Because they're punks," Fleener said. "They didn't try to kill Frank Marshall, did they, Michael?"

"No," I said. "What do you need me for, he knows this stuff?"

"You got more pieces than we do," Hendricks said, "and you're putting them together. What do they tell you?"

"Not sure except we got four bad guys."

"You must have a theory."

"Several theories," I said, "but they don't mean anything and I got no evidence."

"Enlighten us anyway," Hendricks said.

"Give me a couple of days," I said. "I'll know more. Something solid."

I lied. I only had two theories, both weak, neither of which sounded any better after a good single malt scotch than they did right now. But I needed them to give me some room.

Hendricks laced his fingers together, elbows on the desk and rested his chin on his hands. His eyes moved to Fleener.

Fleener shrugged.

"Why did you get Henri LaCroix in this?" Hendricks said.

"Not my idea," I said. "AJ called him."

"AJ?"

"She called him, Don," Fleener said. "Talked to her in the ER."

"Tell him to go back to Mackinac Island," Hendricks said.

I leaned forward in my chair. "First, Don, nobody tells Henri LaCroix what to do. You know that." I leaned back in my chair and smiled. "Besides, you want to argue with AJ?" I looked at Fleener. "You, Marty?"

"LaCroix's trouble," Hendricks said. "That's why we keep an eye on him when he's in Emmet County."

"He's here to help me, Don, not cause trouble for you."

"He's a trained killer, Russo."

"We trained him well," Fleener said. "Our tax dollars at work, gentlemen."

"Blackwater was a private army," Hendricks said. "No tax money there."

"Wanna bet?" I said.

"Doesn't it bother you that's he's a killer?" Hendricks said.

"Not as long as he's on my side."

Hendricks slid his chair back and put his feet on the corner of the desk. He put his hands behind his head and said, "Get outta here, Russo. But we better see you soon. Understood?"

"Understood."

24

I walked out the County building and started down Lake Street. The sun warmed the cool October air as it moved slowly above the trees and over the Bay. Henri LaCroix fell in beside me.

"Thought you didn't want to tag along," I said.

"Over there," he said, pointing to a parking lot across the street. "Didn't want to get picked up for loitering in the County building."

We went down the street and stopped for the light at Howard.

"How'd it go?" he said.

"They don't like you."

"Good to hear," he said. "Must be doing something right."

I laughed. "Not sure Hendricks would agree."

"So, tell me," he said.

I did.

"You really have two theories?"

"Only one, sort of," I said.

"Kellerman and the guys last night are somehow connected."

"That's it."

"Not much of a theory."

"What I got," I said. "Maybe Chicago and DeMio, too. Not sure yet. You find Kellerman?"

"Think so," Henri said.

We went up the stairs to my office.

"See any familiar faces?" Sandy said without taking her eyes away from her screen when we walked in.

"No."

"Too bad," Sandy said.

"A meeting of the brain trust will now convene in my office," I said.

We arranged ourselves in the usual spots around my desk. I undid the cap from a bottle of water and took a long drink.

"You first, Henri. You found Kellerman?"

"I defer to Ms. Jefferies," Henri said, "since we pooled our information. Couple of things to add when she's done."

"Sandy?"

"Okay. Here's what we got," she said. "This includes my stuff and Henri's and Bill Stapleton in Birmingham."

"You talk to Billy?"

Sandy nodded. "He kept trying to talk sports cars," she said. "Very annoying. Kept him on topic, but it wasn't easy. You better call him pretty soon or he's gonna have a stroke."

I laughed. "I'll do that," I said. "Back to Kellerman."

"Found out a little more about Mr. Kellerman. Billy checked him out in Detroit. Nobody really knows him, but he occasionally shows up as second chair or an observer when a mob guy goes to court."

"No kidding," I said. "Who does he work for?"

Sandy shook her head. "No one can say for sure. But he's gotta be mobbed up or why would he show up in court?"

"Good point."

"Better question," Henri said, "why a Petoskey lawyer? The mob can't get good legal advice in Motown?"

I drank the last of the water and put the empty bottle aside for the recycle bin. "We think he's a Petoskey lawyer because that's what he told me. Could be he moonlights up here."

"Remember, he owns property in this neck of the woods," Sandy said.

"You said that before," I said. "Got any details?"

"I do now," Sandy said, looking at the yellow pad in her lap. "The Charlevoix Road parcel is twelve acres, all undeveloped, at the old cement plant."

"You mean Bay Harbor, Sandy?"

"If you say so, boss."

Sandy cleared her throat like she was on stage.

"Not being sarcastic, are we, Sandy?"

"Perish the thought, boss," she said.

"Continue, please."

"The Pickerel Lake Road property he told you about checks out. It's a large house, four bedrooms, two baths on two floors. A pole barn out back. About fifty feet from the road. Easy to spot. It's on Zillow. He rented to a couple in their forties who recently moved from Milwaukee. Both work in town. No connection to Kellerman that I found, other than as lessees."

Sandy flipped to another page of her notes and took a drink of water.

"That leaves Levering. He owns a large lot just outside of Levering."

"Everything's 'just outside of Levering,'" Henri said.

Sandy ignored him. "He's got a trailer on the lot."

"You mean a modular home?" I said.

"I mean a trailer," Sandy said. "It's pretty beat up. Big yard. Lots of weeds. Can't see it from the road. Got a banged up mailbox stuck in the ground next to an overgrown driveway."

"How'd you find all that out?" I said.

"Had a look for myself," she said. "While you were gone."

"You go girl," Henri said and clapped his hands.

"Don't encourage her," I said.

"Any sign of activity?" Henri said.

"Not really," she said. "Maybe some tire marks up by the trailer. Not sure."

"Not much to go on," I said.

"No," Sandy said and put her pad on the desk. "He certainly doesn't live on his own properties."

"Henri? You had something to add."

"Yep," he said. "Mr. Kellerman is a frequent guest at the Perry Hotel. Under a name not his own."

"Then how do you know it's him?" I said.

"One of the many reasons I'm fond of the Perry is my fondness for a very smart, very attractive woman employed by the hotel. Known her about three years."

"She's in a position to know it's our James Kellerman?"

Henri nodded. "Won't talk about her or what she does, but I trust her. It's the only business question I've ever asked her." Henri leaned forward, elbows on his knees. He smiled.

"One more thing," he said. "You're gonna like this one."

"If you say so."

"A few months ago, April or May, I think it was. Mr. Kellerman had to check out unexpectedly. Asked my friend to forward a letter he was expecting at the hotel as soon as it arrived. Gave her a manila envelope with stamps and addressed to him at Zip Code, 49757."

"That's Mackinac Island," I said.

"It gets better," Henri said. "P.O. Box is 1724."

"You gonna make me ask?"

He nodded.

"I'll bite," I said. "What's 1724?"

"Marquette Park Hotel."

"No shit. Carmine DeMio's hotel."

"Yes, it is."

"Stranger than fiction," Sandy said.

"When you see Joey tomorrow," Henri said, "you should ask about Mr. Kellerman."

"Yes, I should." I looked at my watch. "Got time to call Frank."

"Tell him about his brother?" Sandy said.

I nodded. "I wanted to run out there, but Ellen said he'd pushed himself the last couple of days."

"Not being a good patient?" Sandy said.

"No," I said. "He tries to do too much, too fast."

"I hope Frank's got something to add," Henri said.

"Me, too."

"Want me to get him on the landline?" Sandy said.

"Please," I said.

"That's my cue," Henri said. "I'll catch up with you later."

Henri went down the stairs as Sandy stuck her head in.

"Line two, Michael."

I nodded and picked up the desk phone.

"Afternoon, Frank," I said, "I hear you been doing too much, too soon."

"That's Ellen's opinion," Frank said, with a touch of irritation. "I'm doing fine. It's just like running, Michael. You got to do a longer run or a faster one if you want to get better."

"If you say so, my friend."

"Now you sound like Ellen," he said.

"I'll take that as a compliment, Frank. Thanks."

He laughed. "Okay, okay. What's going on you wanted to talk? Any news on who tried to kill me?"

"Not directly," I said, "but each piece might make the puzzle clearer."

"Tell me."

"It's about Tom."

"Is he all right?" Frank said. "Something happen to him?"

"He's okay, Frank," I said. "He lives in Arizona. Did you know that?"

"No, I didn't. We haven't . . . haven't heard from him in several years."

I told Frank what Lenny Stern had to say about Tom, Sedona, and Yoga.

"That sounds like my brother, all right," Frank said. "Teaching Yoga and a woman young enough to be his daughter." He was quiet for a minute. "At least that's the Tommy I knew twenty years ago."

"Think he has something to do with the attempt on your life?"

"Ellen told me about her theory, the one she told you," he said. "I've thought about it off and on. It's hard to believe Rick Morgan would stay angry for twenty years. You'd think he'd have tried to kill me at least once in all that time."

"Yes, you would." I hesitated then said, "Sorry for the question, Frank, but do you think Tom might have set it up?"

"The hit on me?"

"Yeah."

Frank was quiet again.

"No, Michael," he said. "Tom didn't try to have me killed. That doesn't work for me. It's difficult enough believing the hit goes back twenty years. Tommy as the man in charge is a big stretch."

"Well, I wanted to tell you what I'd found out and see if it rang any bells."

"I appreciate that, Michael," he said. "Do you have any contact information for Tom?"

I gave Frank what I had and we chatted for a few minutes. He was more interested in talking about getting his running legs back than talking about his brother. He always focused on the positive. Frank was not oblivious of the past, but he was more interested in how it could help him understand the future.

I said good-bye and went out to Sandy's desk. She had her coat on and was stuffing papers into her briefcase. I told her about my call.

"I don't blame him," she said. "His brother's been gone a long time. But I'd hate to think Tom Marshall tried to have his brother killed."

"I'll trust Frank's judgment on that," I said. "I don't want to hazard a guess."

I looked at the small clock on Sandy's desk. "I have to meet AJ," I said. "See you."

25

"So why does Mr. Kellerman of Detroit . . ." AJ said.

"Grosse Pointe."

"Okay, Grosse Pointe." Ever the professional journalist, AJ wore a charcoal business suit, highlighted by a soft pink silk blouse. The skirt fell just above the knee unless she was sitting down, like now on a barstool, then the skirt sat mid-thigh. I happily ogled.

We were at the far end of the long mahogany bar at the City Park Grill. Ernest Hemingway spent many a Northern Michigan night at this bar dreaming up plots for his short stories. Wonder if he ever invented a tale as convoluted as this one?

The October evening was chilly and damp. The streets were wet and brown leaves stuck to the sidewalk. If it got a little colder, we might see the first wet snowflakes of fall.

It was a slow night at the restaurant. Two tables, both four-tops, were busy. That was it except for Henri LaCroix who sat at a two-top by the front window. He had a clear view of the street and the doorway to the room. He sipped draft beer from a tall thin glass and stared out the window. He could have been any man who stopped for a bite to eat after a hard day's work.

"Mr. Russo, Ms. Lester," the bartender said. "Good evening." We've known Margaret Samuels since she moved down here from the UP after a divorce. She shook her head and I knew what was coming. "Does the other guy look as bad as you?" she said. "Haven't seen a shiner like that since the bar in Marquette where the frat boys hung out. Want some ice for that?"

"No," I said, "but thanks."

"What can I get you?"

Meg took our drink order and went to greet two women who had just sat down.

"So why does Mr. Kellerman live in Grosse Pointe, rent a room in Petoskey using a phony name and stay at a Mafia hotel on Mackinac Island?"

"He likes Mackinac Island?"

"Me, too," AJ said, "but there's got to be more to it than that."

"All the women are sexy and the kids are better than average?"

"That's Garrison Keillor's Lake Wobegon, darling," she said, "but you got the words wrong."

Meg put down a glass of wine for AJ and a tumbler of scotch for me.

"Shalom," I said and we clinked glasses.

"Michael," AJ said. "Be serious about this, please. It's getting scarier."

"The last twenty-four hours have been way too serious," I said. "I'd rather you give me the latest on *PPD Wired* while I stare at your legs." Of course, I'd stare at her legs no matter what she talked about. "How are things with the electronic edition, by the way?"

"Better every day, I'm happy to say. I think the important changes are done. For now anyway." She drank some wine and wiped a drop from her lips with an index finger. "Much easier to navigate the site, so we're getting more hits each week. Small increases, but the trend line is clear."

"Good to hear," I said. "Does the boss agree with your assessment?"

"For the most part," she said. "But Maury'll be happier when we make more money."

"Good thing to be happy about," I said.

"I'll drink to that," AJ said, raising her glass. She sipped some wine and put the glass down.

"Michael, should we invite Henri to join us?" she said, nodding in his direction.

"Go ahead, but he'll say no."

"Why?" she said. "We enjoy each other's company."

"Henri's working, AJ," I said. "He may look relaxed over there, but he watches everything that moves. He can't talk to us and do that at the same time."

She was quiet for a moment. "Well, okay." AJ lifted her glass for Meg to see. "You want to eat, darling?"

"Yes," I said. "I'm hungry."

We were reading the menus when Henri came up behind us.

"Evening, AJ," he said.

"Hi, Henri," she said. "Thanks for being here."

"Happy to," he said. "Going to the men's room, Michael. Don't get shot while I'm gone."

"That's not funny," AJ said.

"Not even a small chuckle?" Henri said and smiled.

AJ shook her head slowly. "Do you think we're in danger in here?"

"No," I said.

"Agreed," Henri said. "Outside, after dinner. If at all." Henri nodded and went towards the restroom.

"After dinner, Michael, Really?"

"Probably not," I said. "Lake Street in the middle of town isn't a good place. Too many people even in October."

"Didn't stop them in Mac City."

"Bernie's was more isolated," I said. "Nobody around except for the gas station next door. Even that's half a football field away."

Meg came by and put a wine glass down.

"Ready to order?" Meg said. We did.

"Michael," AJ said, and put her hand on my arm, "I want to hold you right now. Very tight."

I leaned over and kissed her. "That's very sweet," I said. "We're gonna be okay. I'll know more after I talk with DeMio."

"I guess that'll make me feel better," she said.

Meg brought our food. "Enjoy," she said.

We were eating quietly when Henri came over.

"Good dinner, Henri?" AJ said.

"Whitefish," he said. "Can't go wrong."

"Are you leaving?" she said.

Henri shook his head. "I'm here until you're done. What do you two have planned?"

"Michael's place," AJ said. "I'll walk home in the morning. Get ready for work." She picked up her wine. "You won't have to worry about Michael until you go to the Island."

"What time you want to leave in the morning?" Henri said.

"How 'bout nine?"

"Nine it is. I'll meet you in the parking lot."

"We'll take my car," I said.

"I'll be up front until you're ready to go," Henri said and he went back to his window table.

"Let's go home as soon as we're done," AJ said. "You okay with that?"

"Sure."

She leaned over, close to my face. "I want you in a warm bath," she whispered. "See what happens."

"What always happens," I said. "Except for last night."

"This isn't last night."

26

I rolled over, but AJ wasn't there. The clock on the nightstand said 6:15. She came in the bedroom wearing a yellow sweatshirt and baggy sweatpants that matched.

"You awake?"

"Sort of," I said.

"Maybe this'll help," she said and pulled up the front of her sweatshirt. She wore only bare skin underneath.

"Come over here," I said and smiled.

"Nope," she said. "We did that last night. Just wanted to help you wake up."

"You were successful," I said and sat up in bed.

AJ put her clothes from yesterday in a plastic grocery store sack. "Coffee's ready."

"Kiss me good-bye," I said.

AJ came over and leaned down. I put my hand under her sweatshirt and found her right breast.

"Cut that out, Russo. I'm late as it is."

"What about my kiss," I said.

"You blew your chance," she said and laughed. "Make up for it tonight."

"I'll call you when I'm done with DeMio."

"I'm in the office all day."

AJ got to the bedroom door, turned around and came back to me. She leaned over and we kissed.

"I love you, you know."

"I do know," I said. "Love you, too."

I heard the apartment door close. I got up and went for a mug of coffee.

Twenty minutes later, I'd taken a shower, dressed in fresh khakis, a dusty blue polo shirt and Brooks running shoes. The sun was above the trees and the sky was a bright blue. But since we were headed for Mackinac Island, I grabbed a rain parka and a navy sweatshirt with "Peace Frogs" embroidered across the front in bright colors.

Henry wore jeans, a black t-shirt and a loose, dark green windbreaker to cover his hip holster.

I beeped the door locks and Henri put a canvas duffel bag on the back seat. I pulled out of the lot and headed over to Mitchell Street.

"You carrying a Beretta?"

"A .44 Magnum. Beretta's in the bag," he said, nodding towards the backseat.

"A duffel bag? For a pistol?"

"And the cut-down 12 gauge," he said. "Extra shells, too."

"For crissake, Henri," I said, "you're not back in Iraq?"

"Hope not," he said. "You got nice wheels, Russo, a BMW. I ever tell you that?"

"You changed the subject, damn it."

"I did."

"You still don't want to talk about Iraq and Blackwater?"

"Maybe someday, Michael. Maybe not."

I went down Division then north on U.S. 31 to Mackinaw City. Henri was quiet then said, "What about Tom Marshall? Think he's part of this?"

"Not sure," I said, "but I don't think so. The brothers seem detached from each other."

"So that leaves us with DeMio."

"I wanted to plan for the meeting," I said. "Trouble is, I don't know want to focus on."

"The man knows something," Henri said. "I doubt he'd last very long in the Chicago mob if he didn't pay attention."

Traffic was light, so we got to the Shepler's Ferry parking lot in forty-five minutes.

"Guess I just go to the meeting and listen."

"Hard to do," Henri said. "Maybe he'll say something interesting."

"Find out soon enough."

27

The Straits of Mackinac. Breathtakingly beautiful. Every time.

We sat on the port side –left side – of the Wyandot, for a better view of the Mackinac Bridge, its two towers pushing at the blue sky. A short fifteen minute ride later, we slowed to cut the wake in the harbor at Mackinac Island. The beauty of the shoreline, the Victorian cottages on the bluffs, Grand Hotel and Fort Mackinac still welcomed visitors even though the tourist season was almost over. It welcomed us, too, even though we were armed and I had an appointment with a mob boss.

The Wyandot tied up at the dock and we followed the luggage carts off the boat.

"Look who's here," Henri said.

Leaning on the railing was Santino Cicci, one of DeMio's bodyguards, gunmen and all around troublemakers. Cicci was a bit over six feet, about two hundred pounds, and sported a small goatee.

"Think he's waiting for us?" I said.

"Let's find out," Henri said and picked up his duffel bag.

We got to the top of the ramp, and Henri said, "Good morning, Santino. Shoot any tourists today?"

Cicci eyes were covered by thick-framed sunglasses and his face gave no hint of a reaction.

"Might start with you, tough guy," Cicci said.

Henri laughed. He stopped short, forcing several tourists to veer around him. "Have at it, Santino. If you're good enough."

"You here to meet us?" I said.

"Going across," Cicci said. "Boss'll be safe enough from you two."

"Have a nice day, Santino," Henri said with a big grin.

We went up the dock. A large group of seniors sat patiently for the next ferry to the mainland. Except for two dock porters waiting for their hotel's guests, there was little congestion on the street. We walked east on Main Street towards Marquette Park.

"Did you want to antagonize Cicci?" I said.

"You bet," Henri said and smiled.

"DeMio must not be worried about us," I said, "if we don't need an escort to his office."

"Joey knows why you're here, Michael. You're no threat today."

"No need for you to tag along then."

"I'll stop at the shoe store and see Fran," Henri said. "Meet you at the hotel later."

Henri said good-bye when we came to Astor Street.

"Say hello to Fran for me," I said. Henri waved and kept on walking.

At Doud's corner, I cut across the grass to the curved driveway in front of the Marquette Park Hotel, up the steps and into the lobby. I hung my rain jacket at the door.

I waited for a young couple, likely in their early twenties, to finish checking in. They held hands and were very excited.

"Enjoy your visit to Mackinac Island and congratulations," said the Jamaican woman behind the desk.

"Good morning, sir," she said to me. The woman wore a blue blazer with the hotel's crest embroidered on the breast pocket.

"Michael Russo. Mr. DeMio's expecting me."

She picked up the phone. "Mr. Russo to see Mr. DeMio." A moment later, "You may go in, sir." She pointed at the hallway just down from the desk.

"Thank you," I said. "I'll knock first."

She smiled. "Very good, sir."

I walked the twenty paces to the only door in the hallway. I knocked but didn't wait for a response. I let myself in.

"Come in, counselor," Joey DeMio said from behind his desk. He did not get up to greet me. Some manners. Carmine DeMio and Carlo Vollini sat opposite each other in matching loveseats in front of the fireplace.

Carmine stood. "Michael," he said.

"Good morning, Carmine," I said. I nodded at Vollini and went to the desk. "Joey."

"Sit down," Joey said, pointing to the dark wood chair in front of his desk. Carmine sat back down.

"What happened to you, counselor," Joey said, "run into a door?" He chuckled like he'd told a familiar joke.

I doubt DeMio sent the two guys after me, but I wanted to push.

"Ran into a couple of your punks," I said. "Tried to rough me up at Bernie's the other night." Joey shot a quick glance at Carmine. Joey was surprised, and the glance showed it.

"You oughta hang out at a better class bar."

"I'll keep that in mind," I said. "What you got for me?"

"Information, as you requested," Joey said. "Carlo."

Vollini picked up a manila folder from the coffee table. He was a big man, about six-six and more than two hundred soft pounds. He came over next to the desk and opened the folder.

"Richard Morgan of Chicago ran Morgan Imports, a successful restaurant supply business started by his father. He assumed control of the . . ."

"Carlo," Joey said. Vollini looked up. "Skip that stuff. Get to it." Vollini hesitated and glanced at me.

"Carlo," Carmine said, "we have great respect for your discretion. Do as Joseph says."

Carlo nodded and went back to his notes.

"Richard Morgan, called Rick, died in February, 2009. Of natural causes, according to the death certificate and Harry Gabriel, attorney for Vincenzo Baldini."

"The same Baldini family you work for?" I said.

"In a manner of speaking," Joey said.

I shook my head. "Not good enough, Joey," I said. "Were you and Morgan working together or not?" This would be tougher if they were.

Joey scratched his chin, then his left temple. "We had interests in common."

"In other words, yes," I said.

He ignored me. "Carlo."

"Morgan's estranged wife, Clare, died in July of this year." I did a quick calculation: three months before the attack on Frank Marshall.

"Since 1993, Clare Morgan lived in a small apartment on Chicago's North Side. She never moved back in with her husband. Their only contact came because of their son, Phillip. In effect, they shared custody without benefit of divorce. Phillip was born in 1978, making him thirty-six or seven."

Vollini closed the folder, handed it to Joey, and went back and sat down.

Joey put the file on the desk and folded his hands on top of it. He added nothing. Neither did Carmine.

I leaned forward. "That's it?"

"What did you expect?" Joey said.

"I expected help," I said. "I'm calling in my favor, Joey."

"Michael." It was Carmine. I looked over. "A moment."

Carmine stood and so did Vollini. "Carlo," Carmine said. Vollini nodded and left the room.

Carmine came over to the desk. "Michael, Joseph never liked my debt to you. He still believes it is his debt. The weight of it rests heavy."

"I know that," I said, "but I need to know about the hit on Frank Marshall."

Carmine gestured at Joey and returned to the loveseat. Joey opened the manila folder, and shuffled a few pages.

With no expression and in a flat voice, he said, "Richard Morgan always blamed Frank Marshall for Clare leaving him. As long as Clare was alive, she demanded that no harm come to Marshall. Phil took on that hatred after his father died, but obeyed his mother's wishes. When his she died a few months ago, Phil ordered the hit."

"Were the shooters local? Petoskey or Traverse City? The Island?"

Joey shook his head.

"Chicago?"

"No."

"Detroit?"

Joey shook his head again.

"Do I gotta run the top twenty cities?"

"West Coast," Joey said. "L.A."

"So Phillip Morgan buys two shooters from La-La Land to settle a score for his old man in Petoskey?" I said. "Is that it?"

Joey nodded. He was either lying or not giving me the whole story.

"Who are they?"

Joey shook his head.

"Did Phil Morgan hire them or use somebody else to do it?"

Joey shrugged.

"You know an attorney named Kellerman?"

Joey shook his head.

"All right," I said. "The debt's paid." I stood up. "You're off the hook. You're both off the hook."

I went to the door. "I'll find them with or without your help."

"Remember, counselor," Joey said. "No cops. They'd use a street shooting to get to me. I won't have that."

"Listen, Don Joey," I said. "I'll get them myself. Understand? This is my debt to my friend. You understand a debt, don't you Joey? And I'll get Morgan, too."

Joey stood up for the first time since I got there. He came around the desk and put his hands on his hips. "Counselor," he said, "you understand something. The men from L.A? They're all yours, but stay away from Phil Morgan."

"What do you care?" I looked at Carmine then back at Joey. "What difference does it make to you?"

"We have business with Morgan," he said. "Do not interrupt it. Consider yourself warned."

"Duly noted," I said and opened the door.

"Counselor," Joey said. I stopped.

"Those men gave you the black eye? If I sent 'em, you'd be dead." He turned around without saying good-bye. More bad manners.

I picked up my rain jacket at the front door and left the hotel. The air had grown chilly and the wind came out of the east. Gray clouds hung low over the harbor and promised rain.

"Michael." It was Henri sitting in an old, white Adirondack chair on the porch. "Still alive, I see."

"For now."

28

Henri and I walked Main Street to the ferry dock. The resort season on Mackinac was almost over. In the first block alone, one hotel and three small shops had closed. The crowded sidewalks of summer gave over to very few visitors gazing into shop windows. They wore heavy coats against the damp wind.

"Tell me about Joey," Henri said.

I did.

"Not much to go on," he said.

"Nope."

"Except you annoyed Joey."

"Yep."

"Think he knows more than he's telling?"

"Yep."

"Think he knows Kellerman?"

"Yep."

"You gonna add anything more enlightening than 'yep' and 'nope?'"

"Nope," I said, "unless I have something to add."

"And you don't."

"Nope."

We reached the dock in time for the next ferry. The line was short, perhaps a dozen adults. We climbed aboard and sat down in the back row. The boat eased its way out of the harbor and picked up speed when it the neared the breakwater.

"What do you know?" Henri said, emphasizing the word, "do."

"Same as you," I said.

"That's not much."

"It's not, but I know one thing. Kellerman's the only guy who might be connected to somebody else in all of this."

"Might be connected?"

I nodded. "Better than not connected."

"Think he's involved in the hit?"

I shrugged. "Find him and we'll ask him."

The ride across the Straits of Mackinac was smooth for an October day. When summer eases into fall, the winds in the narrow passage that separates Michigan's two peninsulas can make for an unpleasant trip. Despite the wind, the waves were small and without whitecaps.

Back in Mackinaw City, we walked to the far end of the Shepler's parking lot. Henri weaved in between parked cars about twenty feet to my right and watched carefully. His jacket was unzipped. I beeped the door locks on the 335. Henri put the small duffel bag on the back seat and we climbed in.

Traffic was light on U.S. 31 south. Commuters were still at work and there weren't any more tourists here than on the Island. A light rain hit the windshield hard enough to trigger the wipers.

"Does Frank Marshall know about Phil Morgan and his father?" Henri said.

"Doubt it," I said. "Ellen never told me that Rick or his wife were dead. She just figured revenge had a long reach."

"All the way to Petoskey," Henri said, "twenty years later."

"Uh-huh."

"Maybe you should tell Marshall what we know."

"That still isn't very much, Henri."

"We know Phil Morgan ordered the hit," Henri said. "Ellen Paxton called it right."

"Close enough," I said.

I passed up the turn at Division and stayed on 31 through Bay View. Easy to do this time of year with so little traffic. The rain fell harder now.

The dark sky blended with the water of Little Traverse Bay. I waited for the oncoming traffic to clear at Lewis, turned and went to my parking lot.

"You have a plan for tonight, Michael?"

"I'll be all right, Henri," I said. "You must have something better to do tonight."

"Sure, but you're a pretty exciting guy, Russo," he said. "Live in Petoskey, visit Mafia bosses on Mackinac Island . . ."

"Enough, already."

"Okay," he said, "but what's the plan?"

"Want to go to the office, but I'll call AJ first."

I took out my iPhone and tapped her number. I tapped the phone for speaker and put it on the dashboard.

"Hi, there," AJ said. "Did Butch Cassidy and the Sundance Kid have fun shooting up Mackinac Island?"

"You're on speaker, AJ," I said. "Henri's here."

"Can I be Butch Cassidy this time?" Henri said.

"No," AJ said, emphatically. "You're Sundance or you're out of the movie."

"Slow day at the office, dear?"

"Always time to mess with you, darling," she said with more than a touch of sarcasm.

"Henri wants to know what we're doing this evening, in case he and his pet shotgun have to follow us around."

"Thought we'd eat in," she said. "You can come, too, Henri."

"No, thanks, AJ," Henri said. "Thought I might have drink with a friend after I put you two away for the night."

"Your woman friend who works at the hotel?"

"Yeah."

"Going to the office for a while," I said. "Check in with Sandy and call Frank, tell him what we've learned."

"Are you going to tell me?" AJ said.

"How about in front of the fireplace with a glass of wine?"

"Okay," she said, "gotta go." The line went dead.

We got out of the car. Henri took his duffel bag.

"I'll hang back on the way to the office," he said. "See if we're clear. Grab a coffee while you do your thing."

"Okay," I said.

"I'll make sure you're safe at AJ's later then take off."

"Still think they'll make a run at us?"

"Sooner or later," Henri said. "Sooner or later."

29

"Henri's right, Michael," Sandy said. "Not much to go on."

We were in the office. Sandy was at her desk. Henri sat by the window that looked out on Lake Street, sipping a drink from Roast & Toast. The rain came down hard. A few people scampered from shop to shop, hiding under awnings when they could.

"What ya got there?" Sandy said, pointing at Henri's drink.

"Latte."

"Yum, maybe I'll go down and get one."

"Go ahead," I said. "I'm gonna call Frank."

"Maybe he can add something about the Chicago people," Sandy said.

"Hope so," I said.

"Be right back."

Sandy grabbed her wallet, a huge green and white umbrella with a Michigan State block "S" on it and went downstairs. I sat at my desk and called Frank and Ellen on their home phone.

"Michael," Ellen said. "Always good to hear your voice."

"Me, too, Ellen," I said. "How's he doing?"

"Good, Michael. Frank's strength isn't all back yet, but he moves pretty well, especially considering his age. He eats like a horse, so his weight's coming back, too."

"That's nice to hear," I said.

"Only thing that makes Frank crabby is not running. Doctor won't clear him yet. Could be as soon as tomorrow."

"I understand that one," I said.

"I know you do," Ellen said. "He walks the treadmill every morning. I haven't caught him yet, but I'd bet ten bucks he's tried to run on it."

"What I'd do if I were him," I said and laughed.

"For Pete's sake, don't encourage him," Ellen said.

"I'll shut up," I said. "Promise."

I explained to Ellen what I had in mind.

"Good idea, Michael," Ellen said. "You never know what Frank might remember about the whole episode with his brother and Morgan. Besides, he'd be an investigator again. He's been a good patient, but he's tired of it."

"All the better," I said, "if it helps his recovery."

"Could you and AJ come to dinner tomorrow? It'd be like old times," Ellen said. "Eat food, drink wine and talk about bad guys."

"You don't have to go to that much trouble, you know."

"Happy to do it," she said. "Payback for that lousy hospital food you ate. Seven o'clock okay?"

"Yes," I said. "Let me check with AJ, make sure she's clear. I'll send you a text."

"All right," Ellen said. "See you tomorrow."

I put the phone down and went out to Sandy's office. I sat in the other client chair by the front window. The rain had eased up but few people ventured out. I tapped a message to AJ to check her schedule.

"We're going to Marshall's house for dinner tomorrow, Henri. Fill him in," I said. "Think you'll need to tag along?"

"Get you inside the hallowed walls of Cherokee Point," he said. "You ain't safe with all those gun-loving snobs, you ain't safe anywhere."

"A little cynical, don't you think?" I said.

Sandy rolled her eyes and shook her head.

"What?"

"Nothin' boss," Sandy said. "Far be it for me to criticize the 'Grand Poobahs' of Cherokee Point."

"Grand Poobahs?"

"Gilbert and Sullivan," Henri said, grinning. "*The Mikado.*"

"You had time for opera in Iraq?" I said.

"Iraq was opera, Michael."

My phone chirped. I swiped the screen. AJ was clear for dinner. I texted Ellen.

"AJ's gonna pick me up here in a half hour and we'll go to her house. That okay, Henri?"

He nodded. "Make sure you're tucked in then I'll go."

"Any news on finding Kellerman?" I said to both of them.

Henri didn't respond.

Sandy shrugged but said, "Bill Stapleton called back."

"He want me to call?"

Sandy shook her head. "Nothing new about fast cars so he didn't need to talk to you."

"Heard that before," I said.

"He had a guy sit on Kellerman's PO Box. In Grosse Pointe." Sandy looked up from her notes. "Stapleton said you owe him for the guy's fee."

"Uh-huh."

"Said he'd take a weekend at the Highlands when ski season gets here."

"I bet he would," I said.

"After three days, a man showed up took some mail and left."

"They roust him?" Henri asked.

"They did not," Sandy said. "They were instructed to get a detailed description and that's all. Matches the guy who came here bearing threats."

"License plate?"

Sandy nodded. "Illinois. Cook County."

"That's Chicago," I said.

"Car's registered to," she glanced at her notes, "Morgan Imports."

"That's Phil Morgan's company," I said.

"And his father's company before that," Henri said.

"And always the Baldini crime family."

"Small world," she said. "Anyone believe in coincidences?"

Henri shook his head. I said nothing.

"Didn't think so," Sandy said.

"One more piece links Kellerman to this mess," Henri said.

"All but guarantees Joey DeMio knows Kellerman."

"Yes, it does," I said. "Gotta find that man. Fast."

"Hard to pin down, Michael. He's on the move a lot," Sandy said. "Detroit, Petoskey, Chicago."

"Would your friend at the Perry tell you if he showed up?"

Henri nodded. "Only favor I've asked," he said. "Other than a couple exciting sexual maneuvers." He smiled.

"Really?" I said. "Do tell."

"No. Don't tell," Sandy said.

"Aw, you're no fun. How about just one?" I said, looking at Henri.

"She does this thing," He said, lifting both arms over his head.

"Henri," Sandy said. "This isn't the dorm and you certainly aren't a college boy anymore. That goes for you, too, Mr. Russo."

My phone chirped. "Saved by the bell," I said.

"I'll say," Sandy said.

I read the text, got up and looked out the window. "AJ's double parked," I said, pointing down at Lake Street. "Grab your shotgun, Henri, and let's go."

I put on my jacket, took my brief bag and headed for the door.

"Maybe you'll get lucky and have a line on Kellerman by morning," I said to Sandy.

"Uh-huh," she said. "Maybe you two hotshots will get lucky and grow up by morning."

30

Henri honked the horn as he backed out of AJ's driveway.

"Made it safe and sound," I said, "all the way to your kitchen."

"That's not something to joke about, sweetheart," AJ said. She looked wonderful, but I always thought that.

"You haven't kissed me," she said.

"I was waiting for the right moment."

"It's always the right moment to kiss me, Russo," she said, and put her arms around my neck and pulled me to her. Tight. We kissed, softly at first, then harder.

She let go. "That's better," she said. "Got to change clothes. Wine's in the fridge. Cheese, too. Meet you at the fireplace."

When AJ began restorating her house seven years ago, she insisted on a wood-burning fireplace. Her only concession was a gas starter. I opened the flue and lit the starter. I took three logs from a large brass bucket that sat on the hearth and put them on the flame. Her house felt more removed from downtown than my apartment even though it was only four blocks away. AJ claimed the space as hers, but I always felt welcome and at home. Especially in front of a fire on a chilly fall night.

"That's better," AJ said. Dropping herself on the couch. She'd put on an oversized dark green cotton sweater with a deep V-neck over a pair of black running tights. She'd brushed her hair and the makeup was gone. "Wine, s'il vous plait."

"With pleasure, mademoiselle," I said and poured wine in both glasses.

AJ raised her glass. "A toast."

"To?"

"To being here. Us. In front of the fireplace."

"Amen to that," I said, and we touched glasses.

"Life at the paper still okay?" I said. "Still making progress?"

"Better than okay, for the most part," AJ said. "I think the big speed bumps are behind us. Tuning up the online edition should have been easy in today's techy world . . ." she shook her head, "but no such luck."

AJ broke off a piece of cheese and put in her mouth.

"I've interviewed three people," she said. "One was an especially a sharp woman with two years at the *St. Ignace News*. She came from MSU's J-school."

"Go Green." I said, and raised my glass. "Would she work under you?"

"If Maury signs off on it," she said. "He gets that we need another person, but he's the boss with the budget."

I cut a piece of cheese and took a bite.

"Hope it works," I said.

AJ nodded. "I assume we're on for dinner at Marshall's tomorrow?"

"Yep," I said and drank some wine. "At seven."

"You want to fill me in or make me wait until dinner tomorrow?"

"Might keep you in suspense," I said.

"Perhaps I could tease it out of you."

"Depends on the tease."

AJ yanked the front of her sweater down under both breasts. "This work?"

I leaned over and gently kissed her left nipple. Her chest moved, just a bit. "That work?" I said.

AJ smiled. "Yes," she said and pulled her sweater back in place. "I want some more cheese first."

"Fair enough," I said.

"You might as well fill me in while I munch."

"Okay." I started with Joey DeMio on Mackinac Island and finished with lawyer Kellerman on Mackinac Island.

"For such a small island, Mackinac sure is a busy place for bad guys," AJ said.

"Probably has less to do with the Island than with DeMio," I said. "First Carmine bought the Hotel and then the cottage on the East Bluff." I spiked another piece of cheese. "Then Joey took over the family business, so they're both there, at least during the season."

"You sure the attorney's involved?"

"Uh-huh," I said. "Just not sure how yet."

"Henri think that, too?"

"He does," I said.

"Got another question for you, Michael."

"Okay."

AJ took hold of her sweater at the bottom and pulled it straight over her head. She tossed it on the floor next to the couch. She picked up her glass, sat back and said, "When're you going to kiss my right nipple?"

"Thought you wanted more cheese?"

"I ate more cheese," she said. "Weren't you watching?"

"I was daydreaming."

"Daydreaming?"

"About your body," I said. "About doing erotic things."

"Russo, I'd settle for a kiss on my right nipple. You know, the one right here," she said and pointed. "Hurry up or I'm gonna hit you over the head with the wine bottle."

I leaned over and kissed her right nipple. Then back to the left side.

"Do that thing with your tongue," she said.

"On your nipples?"

"You can start there," she said softly and laid her head back.

31

AJ was still asleep. I escaped the bedroom without her waking up. I went to the kitchen, put ground coffee into the Mr. Coffee, added eight cups of water and pushed the button.

I went into the living room while the coffee cooked. My iPhone weather said it was forty-two and clear. A good morning as October edged towards Halloween. Bay Street was quiet. I didn't expect to see Henri's SUV parked at the end of the driveway but there it was. I hit contacts and punched his number.

"Morning, Russo," he said.

"Coffee's ready."

Henri's phone went dead and he climbed out of the passenger side.

I poured two mugs of coffee and we sat at the kitchen table.

"You out there all night?" I said.

"Not a chance," he said. "Left my car here so the bad guys would think so."

"You walk to the Perry?"

Henri nodded.

"Anybody see you?"

He drank some coffee and said, "You're kidding right?"

"Sorry," I said. "Dumb question."

"Indeed."

"I suppose you want to know my schedule for today?"

"If you got one."

I nodded. "The office. All day," I said. "I've let things slide. Have to catch up before AJ and I go to Marshall's."

"I'll get you to the office in one piece," Henri said. "Got errands to run, make few calls. Be back late afternoon."

I nodded. "Only need a half hour at home before I pick up AJ."

I got up to pour more coffee. "Want some?"

Henri shook his head and I filled my mug.

"Everything okay on the Island?" I said. "You been gone a long time."

He shrugged. "Mostly, yeah," he said. "Got a tenant in a two-bedroom's always late with rent. Might be time to scare him some."

"Really?" I said. "That actually work?"

"It does when I pull my jacket back."

"Don't tell me you threaten to shoot 'em?"

"Only if I have to," he said and laughed. "Sight of a big .44 usually does the trick."

I looked at my watch. "Time to go. Think I can walk to my apartment to change without you shadowing me?"

"Probably," Henri said. "I'll leave now. Be a block ahead of you." He put his mug in the sink and started for the door.

"Be right there," I said. "I want to say good-bye to AJ."

I went to the bedroom and quietly opened the door. She was tucked under the covers and sound asleep. All I could see were curls of black hair. No point waking her up. I eased the door shut. I put her iPhone on the kitchen counter and texted that I'd pick her up at six-thirty. Her phone lit up and buzzed softly. She'd read it when she got coffee.

I went outside and started down the street. Henri's SUV was a good fifty yards ahead. The sun cut through the trees creating a zig-zag pattern on the front yards along the street. It'd be a good time for a run, but I'll settle for a brisk ten-minute walk home this morning. Henri moved slowly down the hill, keeping ahead of me. When I got to Howard, I waved at Henri and went right towards my building. He tapped the horn once and kept going. He'd wait in the parking lot behind the office.

32

The sun was above the buildings along Lake Street by the time I left my apartment. It would hang in the sky all day and get to the low sixties. The humidity of summer was gone. We'd have more days like this, all the way to Thanksgiving if we were lucky. I went up Howard and across the parking lot to Henri's SUV. He got out and pointed to a black sedan a few cars down.

"Cops?"

"Fleener."

"You see him?"

He nodded. "Went into Roast & Toast. Hasn't come out."

"Maybe he's having a Denver wrap for breakfast."

"Don't think so," Henri said.

"Me either," I said. "Probably went out the front."

"Bet he's upstairs chatting with Sandy."

"Let's find out."

We walked up the stairs and into the office.

"Good morning," Sandy said. She held up a cinnamon donut and pointed it at my office. "We have company."

I put my coat on the rack at the door.

Captain Martin Fleener sat at my desk, in my chair, smiling.

"Gentlemen." Fleener stood up and extended his arms with an exaggerated gesture at the box on the desk. "From Johan's," he said. "Fresh baked goods for your morning coffee."

He walked around the desk and sat in the client chair. Henri sat in the chair on the sidewall.

"Ms. Jeffries was kind enough to offer me coffee," he said raising a mug. "Bet she'd get you some if you asked nice."

We didn't have to ask at all. Sandy appeared at the door. She handed one mug to Henri and put mine on the desk.

"What have we got?" I asked and opened the box. "Geez, Marty, a lot of carbs?"

"Could be here a while," he said. "Wouldn't want you to go hungry."

"A while?"

"Got a few questions," Fleener said. He looked over at Henri. "For both of you."

I took an almond Danish and Henri picked up a pecan roll. I bit off a nice chunk.

"Good carbs," I said. "One of the basics."

Fleener let the humor slide. He chose a jelly donut and drank some coffee.

"Last time we talked about the Marshall investigation," he said, "was the day you spanked Hendricks and me for getting nowhere. Remember?"

"Of course, I remember," I said. "Doing any better?"

Fleener put his hands out, palms up. "I didn't come here to piss you off, Michael. We're still on it, but I know you been poking around. Anything we should know?"

"I'd tell you, Marty."

"Of course, you would," Fleener said. He looked in the Johan's box. "Your talk with DeMio any help?"

I hesitated and drank some coffee. "You following me, Marty?"

Fleener shook his head. "How many times I have tell you, Russo, it's not you." He nodded in Henri's direction. "It's Mr. LaCroix, here. Or should I call you Major LaCroix?"

Henri didn't react to Fleener's crack. He ate more Danish instead.

"Henri comes off the Island, goes south of the bridge, we get him. St. Ignace or the Sault office keeps an eye on him in the UP. No offense,

Henri," Fleener said. Henri nodded. "But trouble naturally follows you around."

"Got a reputation," Henri said and smiled.

"You certainly do," Fleener said. He picked up his mug. "DeMio have anything to say?"

"Plenty," I said. "Just nothing helpful."

"Want to let me decide that for myself?"

I shrugged.

"He know about the guys gave you the shiner?"

"Seemed to," I said.

"Say who hired them?"

I shook my head.

"Think he knows?"

"I do," I said.

"Think anything happens around here he doesn't know about?"

"I doubt it. He's got reasons to know."

"Awfully generous, Russo," Fleener said. "Any idea what those reasons might be?"

"Family business, be my guess," I said.

"Mine, too," Fleener said, "but I need more than guesses."

I nodded.

"You got anything helpful to add, Henri?"

Henri smiled. "Johan's pretty good stuff, Captain."

"That it?"

"Uh-huh."

"Thought so," Fleener said.

Sandy leaned on the doorjamb.

"What's up?" I said.

"See you a minute, Michael?"

I got up. "Be right back."

Sandy went to her desk in the front office. "Ray Elkins just called," she said. "Thought you'd want to know."

"Okay."

"He's got Laurie Wiecek and her boyfriend, Garner, in the Cedar County jail."

"Seriously?"

"Uh-huh. Said he'd hold 'em twenty-four hours. He wants paperwork or he'll let them go."

"Thanks," I said. I went back to my desk and sat down.

"Anything wrong?" Henri said.

"No," I said, "quite the opposite. Sheriff down in Cedar County . . ."

"That Ray Elkins?" Henri said.

I nodded. "He's got my missing woman and her boyfriend."

"That the guy ripped off Bernie's Bar?" Fleener said.

"Yep." I sat back, put my hands behind my head. "I need some help, Marty."

"Anything, Michael," he said. "Help any way I can. You being so helpful to the investigation and all."

"Goddamn it, Marty, give the sarcasm a break, will ya?"

"Maybe," Fleener said. "What d'ya need?"

"Guy that runs Bernie's, Malone, won't file charges against Eddie Garner or Laurie Wiecek."

"Because?"

"Malone wants 'em," I said, "so the good ole boys give 'em a wuppin'. Or worse for the woman."

Fleener picked up his coffee mug and drank some. He glanced in the Johan's box, but resisted the temptation.

"What d'ya have in mind?"

"If I can convince Malone to call the Mac City cops and file charges against Garner . . ."

"You just said he wouldn't do that."

"Right," I said, "but if I can convince . . ."

"How you gonna do that?" Fleener said.

"Leave that to me, Marty, but if Malone files charges against both of them, will you get the woman off the hook? With the cops?"

"Why?"

"Plenty of people like Pam Wiecek get in a jam. Don't know where to turn. She came to me. That's all. Want to get her sister back in one piece. Don't care about Garner."

Fleener looked at his watch. "Getting late," he said. Fleener stood up, rearranged his suit jacket. "Mac City cops are reasonable guys," he said. "I'll reach out. Or Hendricks will. It's Emmet County, after all."

"Thanks," I said. "I'll let you know."

"You do that," Fleener said. "But."

"But what?" I said.

"This is a trade, not a favor," he said.

"What do you want?"

"I want what you know about the shooting," he said. "I'll get the woman off, but I want to know or it's no deal."

"Okay," I said. Maybe I lied, maybe not. Didn't say I wouldn't edit what I'd say.

"Call me," Fleener said. He turned and went out of the office. I heard him say good-bye to Sandy.

"You gonna tell him everything?" Henri said.

I shook my head. "Won't have to," I said. "This'll be all over 'for I have to do that."

"You're an optimist."

"A 'cockeyed optimist,' to be precise."

"Now you're doing Nellie Forbush? Mitzi Gaynor?"

I shrugged. "Want a beer?"

"I'd rather have another pecan roll."

"Can't get a pecan roll at Bernie's," I said.

"Who's goin' to Bernie's?" Henri said.

"We are," I said and smiled. "Want to reconsider that beer."

Henri shook his head. "Rather cause trouble." He smiled. "Seems I got me a reputation."

33

"You got no idea how to convince Malone to file charges against Garner, do you?" Henri said. He drove his SUV up 31 towards Mackinaw City. We'd passed Alanson on the way to Pellston.

"Watch your speed, will you?" I said. "Don't need any more attention from the cops."

"My speed?" Henri said. "This from the man who races his three hundred horse, twin-turbo BMW around the back roads of the UP? You want me to watch my speed?"

"That's different," I said.

"Would Mario Andretti be so kind as to explain?"

We passed the airport at Pellston. The parking lot was full. Like always.

"I do it for fun. You drive because you have to. Besides you're not paying attention to how fast you're going."

Henri laughed. "In a hurry to get to Bernie's," he said. "Can't wait to see how you're gonna deal with Malone."

"Patience, my friend, patience."

Traffic was light and the trip was uneventful. Henri eased his big SUV into the parking lot at Bernie's. The neon sign was not lit, but a small, phony neon "open" sign hung at an odd angle in a window.

"Place's still a dump," I said.

"That's reassuring," Henri said.

"What is?"

"Lot a change in the world. Nice to know something's the same."

"Even Bernie's?"

"Especially Bernie's."

Three trucks were parked near the door. Henri went past them and backed into a spot on the far side of the lot. He turned off the motor and put the key in his jacket pocket.

"How you want to play this?" he said.

"I'll go in first," I said. "Wait a few minutes then come in easy."

"Easy? That's no fun."

"Easy," I said. "Maybe Malone will play nice."

"Wanna bet?"

"No," I said. "But I want to try."

I left my jacket on the seat and closed the door.

Bernie's Bar was still a basement of a room. Not that I expected a makeover since my last visit. Shane Malone was behind the bar, moving glasses around. He looked up and I could tell he was trying to place me. Four men, probably in their forties, sat at a table on the other side of the room. They watched me, too.

"Hi, ya, Shane," I said and walked toward him. "I'm back."

"Thought I told you to stay outta here." Guess he recognized me.

"Is that any way to treat a paying customer?"

"Turn around and get out," he said. "Or the boys here," he nodded at the table, "will throw you out."

I glanced at the men. "Hi, guys," I said and kept moving.

I sat down on a stool in front of Malone. "Got news you might want to hear, Shane."

"You got nothing I want to know." He put down the towel and leaned forward on the bar, arms spread apart.

Before I could say anything else, Henri LaCroix came through the door and walked to a stool at the bar between the table of men and me.

"Howdy," he said, smiling.

"Howdy?" Never heard him say "howdy" before.

Malone looked at Henri then back at me. He wiped his hands on his dirty white apron and started down the bar.

"I got Eddie Garner," I said.

Malone stopped and came back. He stared at me.

"Whaddya mean, you got Garner?"

"Know where he is," I said.

"Where?"

I shook my head. "Not yet. You listen first."

"The hell I will," Malone said. "Don't . . ."

"Hey." It was Henri. "What I gotta do for service around here?"

Malone and the four men stared at Henri.

"Well?" Henri said. "How 'bout some service, pardner?"

"Pardner?" First "howdy," now "pardner?"

Malone walked down the bar.

"What can I get you?"

"A pecan roll," Henri said.

"What?" Malone said.

I pretended to scratch my head. Hard not to laugh.

"A pecan roll," Henri said. "And a little butter."

"Does this look like the Mackinaw Bakery?"

"It most certainly does not," Henri said.

"Order or get out," Malone said.

Henri turned on the bar stool and looked at the four men. "Is he always this friendly?"

One of the men, a round guy, with a puffy face, shaggy beard and nearly bald said, "You some kinda fag, cowboy?"

Henri stared at the man. "Who you callin' a cowboy?"

"What?" the round guy said. "The fuck you talkin' about?"

"Smile when call me a cowboy," Henri said. "I'm not gonna tell you twice."

This must be Henri's idea of coming in easy.

"Malone," I said, but the bartender paid no attention. "Shane Malone." I slammed my fist on the top of the bar, hard.

"Man's calling you, Malone," Henri said, pointing at me. "You tell him yet, Russo?"

"Not yet," I said. "You keep interrupting."

"Well get on with it," Henri said.

"You guys know each other?" Malone said.

"Tell him, will you, Russo," Henri said. "Baldy over here's starting to get on my nerves."

The round man stood up. He was shaped like an over-stuffed pear.

"You," he said, "orange sweater. You a fag, too?"

"Burnt orange," I said. "It's actually burnt orange."

The round man walked up to Henri.

"Stand up," he said.

Henri came off the stool and stood four feet away. The round man was taller than Henri by a good three inches.

He moved forward, reached out and put a fist against Henri's chest. "Get out."

Good thing I didn't blink. I'd have missed it. Henri took the round man's forearm, yanked it down, twisted it, spun him around and shoved him, hard. The round man hit two chairs, an empty table and landed on the floor.

"Careful, Henri," I said.

"Aw, I'm not gonna hurt him," Henri said.

Henri kept his eyes on the round man. "Stay there," he said.

A second man, younger and leaner than his friend on the floor, stood up. "Hold it, Jake," said a third man at the table. "I know this guy," he said. "You Henri LaCroix? Mackinac Island?"

Henri nodded.

"Sit down, Jake," the man said. "You do not want to fuck with this guy. I seen him fight." He shook his head. "Sit down." The man did not sit, but he didn't move either.

"Russo," Henri said, sitting back on the bar stool. "Finish with Malone. It's time to get outta this dump."

"Shane," I said. "Come here."

Malone walked slowly back to me.

"About Garner," I said.

"What about Garner?" he said, but the steam was gone from his voice.

"Give him to the cops."

"Bullshit," Malone said.

"Look," I said, "this is a one-time offer. Call the Mackinaw City police and file charges." Malone started to shake his head, but I cut him off. "Do it my way, or you don't get Garner at all."

"Why you doing this?" he said. Malone regained some of his footing. "What's in it for you?"

"Laurie Wiecek," I said. "She walks away."

"Hell she does," Malone said.

"Call the cops and file charges. Forget the woman or you lose Garner. I'll see to it."

"I'll burn your ass," Malone said. "Yours, too, asshole," he said pointing at Henri. "Five of us. Two of you." Malone folded his arms across his chest and grinned. "What d'ya say now?"

"Five against three," Henri said.

"How you figure?" Malone said.

Henri scratched his head, as if bored by the question. "Well, there's Russo over there. There's me, the asshole. And our friend here." Henri reached under his coat, pulled out his long-barreled .44 Smith & Wesson and put it on the bar. "That makes three."

"You can't do that." It was the guy still standing at the table. "You can't just pull a gun like that. I'll call the cops. See what they say about outsiders with guns."

"Now there's a man who's using his head," I said. "Let's call the cops. How about it, Shane?"

Malone started to say something, but didn't.

I leaned in. In an easier tone, I said, "The woman was along for the ride. Call the cops, you put Garner in jail. Pick up the phone, Shane. Garner's the one you want."

Malone never looked up. He stared at the bar.

"Make the call or I'll get the health department in here. You'll be in an old folks home before this dump serves another burger, beer or basket of fries."

Malone slowly reached for the phone on a shelf next to the cash register.

I got up and walked towards the door.

"You done, Henri?"

Henri picked up his gun. He went over to the table of men. The round man was still on the floor, but the other three were in their seats. He put the gun back in the shoulder holster under his coat.

"Next time a couple of strangers walk in here," he said, "keep your mouths shut."

34

"The health department?" Henri said. We were headed south on 31, back to Petoskey. Traffic was still light. One of the small pleasures of the fall after a busy tourist season. The second hour of Diane Rehm played quietly in the background on Interlochen Public Radio. "You get that from *The Godfather*?"

"Nah. William Kent Krueger. Maybe Robert Parker. Can't remember."

"You want to go back to the office or home?"

"The office," I said. "Didn't get much done this morning."

"What about Fleener?"

"I'll call him," I said. "As soon as I know Malone did the right thing."

"You have to give Fleener something, he gets the woman out."

"Yeah, I know."

"Any idea what?"

"We still don't know that much," I said.

"More than Fleener, Michael."

"True," I said. We caught the light at the Harbor-Petoskey Road, turned left on Division and took Mitchell Street into town.

"He might get lucky and find himself a clue," Henri said.

I looked over at Henri. "You being sarcastic?"

He nodded.

"Even if I tell him what we know, he still needs luck."

"We could use some luck, too," Henri said. "We sort of know what the puzzle looks like. Missing key pieces."

"Like who the shooters are," I said.

"And where they are," Henri said.

"Especially that."

Henri went over to Lake Street and stopped in front of my building. "What time you picking up AJ?"

"Six-thirty."

"Meet you at her house," Henri said.

"Plan on following us?"

"Yeah," he said. "I'll get you to the hallowed grounds of Cherokee Point. Leave you alone 'till after dinner."

"Think I'll be safe out there?"

"Un-huh," Henri said. "Those rich guys got lots of guns. Too scary for a couple of professional assassins."

"See you later," I said and went upstairs to the office.

Sandy was at her desk sipping coffee.

"Hello, Michael," she said. "How was Bernie's?"

I hung my coat at the door and sat in a client chair across from Sandy's desk.

"Didn't eat a Horseburger, if that's what you meant?"

"Glad to hear it," she said. "I meant, tell me about Malone?"

I filled Sandy in on our visit to Bernie's.

"Henri really ordered a pecan roll?"

I nodded. "Would I make that up?"

"Yeah, you would," she said, "but you didn't, did you?"

I shook my head. "Nope."

"Wish I'd been there to see that," she said. "How'd you keep a straight face?"

"Wasn't easy."

"Think Malone'll do want you want?"

I shrugged. "Think so, but we'll see."

"Your mail's on the desk," she said. "No messages."

"Okay," I said, and started for my office.

"Want me to see if I can find out about Eddie Garner and the Wiecek woman?"

"Wait 'till later this afternoon," I said. "If you haven't heard anything, call."

"Okay."

I spent the next few hours working through several files. Most of my clients seemed happy with the attention I was giving them. Good thing, too, because it didn't seem like I'd given them much attention lately.

"Michael," Sandy said from the doorway. "Just got a call from a friend in Mac City. Garner and Wiecek should be back by six o'clock or so."

"Tonight?"

"Yeah."

"Your friend say anything about the charges?"

"Only one charged is Garner."

"Guess I'd better call Marty," I said.

"Good idea," Sandy said. "Keep Fleener happy."

I found his name in my contacts list and swiped the screen on my iPhone.

"What do you want?" Fleener said.

"Is that any way to greet a friend?"

"Yes," he said. "What do you want? I'm busy."

"Busy?"

"Yes, damn it. I'm memorizing lyrics to a Jay-Z video. What do you want?"

"You're not serious?"

"Wanna bet?"

"No," I said. "Thanks for getting Laurie Wiecek off the hook."

"Malone didn't file on her," he said. "I made sure nobody else did either."

"I owe you."

"Damn right," Fleener said. "You're gonna tell me what you know. That was the deal."

"Okay."

"You're buying lunch at Twisted Olive."

"I am?"

"Yes. I'll call you," he said and hung up.

I walked out to Sandy's desk. "You got Pam Wiecek's work schedule at Audie's by any chance?"

"She never gave it to me," Sandy said. "Want her number?"

"Yes."

Sandy pulled a manila folder from a side drawer. "Here," she said and handed me a yellow sticky note.

I nodded, went back to my desk and punched in her number.

"Hello?"

"It's Michael Russo."

"Yes?" She sounded hesitant.

"Good news," I said.

"Really?" Her voice brightened up. "About Laurie?"

"Yes," I said. "You work the Chippewa Room tonight? Or the bar?"

"No," she said. "Worked breakfast in the Family Room this morning. Why?"

"Your sister ought to be back by six or so tonight. At the police station," I said. "Thought you'd like to know."

"Is she okay?"

"Far as I know," I said. "She's free to go. No charges."

"That is good news, Mr. Russo," she said. "I'll pick her up."

"Thought you might like to," I said.

"Thank you, again," she said and we ended the call.

35

I reviewed a few more files, but I'd had enough. Sandy had already gone for the day. I put the files on Sandy's desk and got my coat and brief bag.

I got to my apartment in one piece and sent AJ a message that I was on time.

I put on a fresh pair of pleated khakis and slipped into an old-fashioned pair of penny loafers. Cordovan. Hadn't worn them in years. I clipped the holster to my left hip. It was getting to be a habit. Not sure if I liked it or not.

A few minutes later, I pulled in AJ's driveway. Henri's SUV was at the curb. AJ stood next to the driver's door talking with Henri. She waved and came over to my car.

"He'll follow us to Cherokee Point, make sure we're inside the gate before he heads back," AJ said. She wore a navy V-neck sweater over a pink camisole with appealing cleavage.

I drove over to Harbor Springs, went north out of town to Robinson Road and turned left towards Lake Michigan.

"Is Henri back there?" AJ said.

I glanced in the rearview mirror.

"He keeps close most of the time. But he'll back off near a crossroad. Gives him a better chance to spot something."

I turned onto North Lake Shore.

"Has it been a year since the Abbott murder?" AJ said.

"Just about," I said. "Lot of people at Cherokee Point annoyed by that investigation."

"What did they expect when Abbott turned up with a bullet in the back of his head?"

We'd driven a few miles when I saw three white wooden flagpoles that marked the resort entrance. The flags, one each for the United States, the state of Michigan and Cherokee Point itself, hung lifeless without a hint of wind. I slowed the car, turned in and stopped in front of a large iron gate. Floodlights mounted high in the trees snapped on and lit the entire area around the gate. A fieldstone wall, about six feet high, ran out from either side of the gate into the woods. A small clapboard sided gatehouse stood off to the side, in the trees.

Henri slowed and pulled onto the shoulder of the road. He did not turn in behind us.

The door to the gatehouse opened and a man came out carrying a clipboard. He was in his mid-twenties. He wore khakis and a navy wool coat over a dark colored polo shirt. The coat had "Staff" written in script on the left breast. He watched Henri's SUV as he came up to my car.

"Good evening, sir," he said, looking at me then at Henri.

"Good evening," I said. "Michael Russo to see Frank Marshall. The man back there," I pointed over my shoulder, "will leave when we're inside the gate."

"Very good, sir."

He flipped a page on the clipboard and made a mark.

"Who might the little lady be?" he said.

"I dunno," I said. "Why don't you ask the little lady?"

AJ put her hand on my leg. "He's just doing his job, darling. Take it easy." She leaned over towards the steering wheel and said, "AJ Lester for Frank Marshall."

"Yes, ma'am, thank you." The man made another mark on his sheet. "Do you need directions, sir?"

I shook my head. "Been here before," I said. "Thanks."

The man waved his arm and the iron gate slowly slid open. Someone else was in the gatehouse.

I moved ahead and the gate closed behind me. I looked in the mirror as Henri made a U-turn and went back down the road.

I'd been to Cherokee Point many times over the years, especially since Frank Marshall and Ellen Paxton moved there from Chicago in 1999. Even at dusk, the tranquil beauty of the resort, called the "Point" by residents, was obvious. Manicured lawns, white stone driveways, championship tennis courts, and stately evergreens lent the resort an air of civility, seclusion, and privilege.

Name signs carved in wood sat at the end of each driveway. I turned in at Frank Marshall's sign and stopped in a small parking area. We got out of the BMW and walked up the driveway towards the house, a gray two-story of clapboard and stone. The garage faced the driveway and the front of the house faced Lake Michigan.

"We should have brought a bottle of wine," AJ said.

"You know they don't like that."

"I know," AJ said. "Seems like a nice thing to do, that's all."

"They don't want to keep track of who owes what."

Just then we heard voices. Around the side of the house came Frank and Ellen.

"Greetings," Frank said.

"Welcome," Ellen said. "So good to see you."

We exchanged hugs all around.

"You look like you're moving pretty well," I said to Frank. "No signs of a limp, anyway."

"Ran my first mile this morning," he said with a huge grin.

"You built up to it slowly, I hope?"

"No," he said with a sheepish grin. "But I'll slowly work up to two miles. Pretty good for an almost dead guy in his sixties." He laughed. Ellen didn't laugh.

"Come on," Ellen said. "We've got chilled wine and whitefish dip waiting."

We followed them around the side of the house to a door that led into the kitchen.

"Put your coats there," Ellen said, gesturing at a hall tree next to the door.

The kitchen, like the rest of the house, had been redone when Frank and Ellen made the one-time cottage their permanent home. It was small by modern standards, but updated with all the usual appliances, new glass front cupboards and white paint. They tore out the old carpet and refinished the hardwood floors.

"Go straight to the porch," she said. "We're right behind you."

We walked through the dining room and the living room, each of which was tastefully filled with American antiques. We got to the porch and sat in a white wicker loveseat. Frank turned the porch into a three-season room when he replaced the screens with sliding glass doors. The expanse of Lake Michigan spread out before us as far as we could see. Somewhere behind several soft clouds, the sun had dropped below the horizon. It was almost dark.

Frank carried four glasses and an uncorked bottle of Chardonnay. Ellen put down a tray of crackers and whitefish dip on the coffee table in front of the loveseat.

Frank poured wine in the glasses and sat down in a wicker armchair.

"Don't stuff yourselves," he said. "Dinner'll be ready in a few minutes."

"What's to eat?" AJ said.

"Roasted pork loin," he said, "with redskins and asparagus."

"I'll drink to that," I said and raised my glass.

"Here, here," the others chimed in.

We chatted amiably for a while, sipping wine and snacking on the whitefish dip, before moving to the dining room. It was a small room, like the living room and the kitchen, but it was warmly decorated with an oak table and four high-back chairs, a hutch on a sidewall and a large cut-glass chandelier that hung from the ten foot ceiling. The table was covered with a white linen tablecloth.

Ellen brought a platter from the kitchen and put it front of Frank.

"Are you going to ham it up for our guests, darling?" Ellen said.

"You mean the carving?"

Ellen nodded.

Frank sliced the pork loin and served it with very little fanfare. We helped ourselves to the trimmings.

"All right," Frank said, putting down his fork, "the police had nothing new the last time I asked." He poured more wine into his glass and passed the bottle to me. I did the same. "Have you learned anything?"

"As a matter of fact."

"Do tell," he said and ate some asparagus.

"Early on," I said, "while you were in the hospital, after Ellen told me about Chicago, about your brother and the Mafia woman . . ."

"Clare Morgan," Ellen said.

I nodded. "I did some checking," I said. "Wanted to see what popped."

Frank looked at Ellen.

She shrugged. "It was just a theory, Frank."

"And the theory was?"

"That Rick Morgan wanted to kill you."

"Bit of a stretch, don't you think?" he said.

"You always thought Morgan held a grudge."

"After twenty years? Morgan'd be an old man."

"It was just a gut feeling, darling," Ellen said and drank some wine. "That's all. A gut feeling."

"Well," I said, "it's more than a gut feeling."

Frank and Ellen stopped, as if frozen in place. Their eyes were fixed hard on me. I told them about Joey DeMio. About Chicago. About Rick Morgan. And about hate.

Frank picked up his wine glass, but didn't take a drink. "So Clare kept a lid on revenge all these years?"

I nodded.

"She died and her son, what's the name again?"

"Phil."

"Phil Morgan hired two guys out of L.A. to kill me. Is that it?"

"That's it," I said.

"And they almost did," Ellen said.

"Yes," Frank said. "They almost did." His eyes looked heavy and sad.

AJ got up. "I know most of this," she said. "You all sit. I'll clear the table."

"Do you know any more about the shooters?"

I shook my head. "Not yet, but I will."

"That's more than I can say for the cops," Ellen said. The disgust in her voice was clear.

"Ellen," Frank said, "the cops . . ."

"To hell with 'em, Frank," Ellen said, louder. "They haven't done a damn thing. Leave the cops out of it, Michael. Go after them yourself. Start with Morgan's son."

"Didn't DeMio warn you about Phil Morgan?" Frank said.

"I will go after Morgan if I have to," I said. "Would you be satisfied if we only got the shooters?"

Frank started to say something, but Ellen interrupted. "Well, I wouldn't be satisfied, as you put it. Get 'em, Michael. The son, too. He ordered it. Forget the cops. Kill all of 'em."

"Ellen," Frank said. "That's a little strong, don't you think?"

"Strong, my ass. They left you on the street to die. Give me one good reason why I shouldn't want them all dead. One reason. Maybe I'll listen."

Ellen got up.

"The cops won't kill 'em. I want them dead." She threw her napkin on the table and went to the living room. AJ stood at the doorway. She'd heard the anger. And the fear.

AJ nodded at me and followed Ellen.

Frank and I finished clearing the table, cleaning up the kitchen and loading the dishwasher. We took a small plate of sugar cookies to living room and sat down with AJ and Ellen.

"Sorry," Ellen said, not looking at any of us. She sat leaning forward with her elbows on her knees. "Guess I'm still scared. These guys could come at Frank again. Hell, they made a run at you, Michael."

"Guys that put me in the hospital weren't the shooters, Ellen," I said.

"That doesn't make me feel any better," Ellen said. "So there's four bad guys? Is that what you're telling me?"

"Only two are killers, Ellen," I said.

"I don't give a damn," she said. "Morgan started it. Morgan ordered it. It's just that, well, it's just . . ." Her voice trailed off and she looked at me.

"I'll get them, Ellen," I said. "I'll find them and I'll take care of them."

Ellen nodded and sat back in the chair. "I know you will," she said softly. "Thank you."

The tension in the room slowly faded. We sat peacefully, ate cookies and finished the wine. We changed the subject. We talked of Frank's recovery, how soon he'd run two miles and AJ's work at *PPD Wired*.

"Speaking of the paper," AJ said. "I got an early meeting." She stood up. "Thank you for a lovely dinner. It's always good to see you."

We went to the kitchen and got our coats.

"Keep me up to date, Michael," Frank said.

"Of course," I said. "Tell me when you're ready to do four miles. I'll come out here and run it with you."

"I'd like that very much."

We said goodnight and went out the kitchen door.

36

The night was cool even for October. The sky was clear and the moon put plenty of light on the ground. AJ and I held hands as we went around the side of the house and walked towards the car.

"Shit," a voice said. "Romantic old fuckers."

We stopped. Off the driver's side of the car, twelve feet away, stood two men in their early twenties wearing baggy jeans and plaid flannel shirts. I recognized them.

"The guys from Bernie's," I said to AJ.

"That's us, shithead," said the guy with a shaved head. The other man, a little taller, stood silently, trying to look tough.

"You called me that at Bernie's," I said. I took a step to my left, away from AJ.

"Hold it right there," he said and pulled a .45 automatic out of his jacket pocket. He raised the gun in both hands and pointed it at us.

"What do you want?" I said.

"Gonna teach you a lesson, shithead."

"Isn't that what you did at the Bernie's?"

"You didn't listen, shithead," he said. "Chicago warned you to go away but you kept at it. Now we're gonna hurt you."

"You did that before, too," I said.

He ignored me. "Open your coat," he said. "Slowly."

I pulled back my jacket. He saw my hip holster.

"Get it, Al," he said to the other man.

AJ moved slightly away from me.

"Stop," he said, pointing the gun at AJ. "Another step I put one right between your tits. Got it?"

"Got it," AJ said, as the other man came up to me and reached in at arm's length, like he didn't really want to touch my gun. But he took it anyway.

"Throw it over there, Al." The man tossed my gun in the tall grass off to the side of the driveway.

"Here's how we do this," he said. "Slow. First bullet in the knee. No more jogging for you, shithead."

How'd he know I run? They been watching? Somebody tell them?

"Next one in the balls. Mo more fuckin' the broad, here." He let out a quiet laugh. He was enjoying this. Not a good sign.

I kept my eyes on them, standing side by side. I looked for something, anything, to give me a chance.

I saw the gun first. In the moonlight. Then Henri's face. He stood at the side of the driveway, twenty-five feet behind the two men. Henri went down on one knee. The barrel of his big gun pointed at the four of us. He gestured with the gun, moving it slightly side to side. I knew what he wanted.

"Hey," Henri yelled.

The two men spun around. I grabbed AJ and pushed us out of the line of fire.

Bam. One shot shattered the silence of the night. The noise echoed in the woods.

The man with the shaved head and the gun landed flat on his back, his arms splayed out like a politician waving triumphantly to the crowd.

I walked up and kicked the gun out of his hand. He wouldn't need it again. A dark red stain came through his coat chest high.

"Don't move," I said to the other man. But he was frozen in place by what had just happened.

Henri came up, the gun down at his side. He stopped next to the body and looked down.

"How 'bout that," he said. "Right between the tits."

Henri took two steps over to the other man who looked like a deer caught in the headlights. Henri moved in, close.

"You got anything to say?"

"No, sir."

"Stand still, understand?"

"Yes, sir."

"Until I tell you to move."

"Yes, sir," the man said again as floodlights high on the roof's edge lit up a huge area behind the house.

"Michael?" It was Frank Marshall, still hidden by the side of the house.

"All clear, Frank," I said. "Come on."

Frank and Ellen walked around the corner of the house and over to the car. He looked at all of us, the dead man last.

"Michael?" he said. "You all right?"

I nodded. "You know Henri LaCroix?" I said.

"I do," Frank said.

"Henri," Ellen said. She walked over to the other man who still hadn't moved.

"Did you try to kill my husband?" she said in a voice that was deep, clear and scary.

"No, ma'am," he said, shaking his head vigorously.

"Ellen," I said.

She turned around with a jerking move, as if I'd interrupted something important.

"The kids from the bar, Ellen," I said.

"The ones that beat you up?"

"Yeah," I said.

Ellen took a step back. She pulled out her phone. "I'll call."

"What happened?" Frank said.

"I was about to ask the same question," I said. "Henri?"

"I left you and AJ at the gate," he said. "Headed back to town when I saw a car on the side of the road. About a half mile down. Just enough light in the sky to see two heads in the car."

"These guys?" Frank said.

Henri nodded. "Went a ways down the highway, flipped around came back. The car was still there. The two heads weren't. There was an opening in the woods."

"That's where the cutline is . . . for the power lines. On the edge of resort property," Frank said.

"Found a small trail. Picked the two guys up, followed them here."

"You been waiting all this time?" I said.

Henri nodded. "Had lots of practice." He looked at the dead man. "They got pretty antsy. Thought they were gonna bolt, then you came out." Henri was still talking when a man walked out of the shadows of the house next door. I tensed up.

"Frank?" the man said as he got closer. It was Wardcliff Griswold who lived a few houses down on the resort. I had several run-ins with the well-connected, officious head of Cherokee Point last year. Even in the dark I could tell he was dressed for any occasion, or at least golf at the country club. He wore dark cord pants and a tan wool sweater. The collar on his navy pea coat was turned up.

Frank turned around. "Ward. What are you doing here?"

"Got a call from the gate. Apparently the police are on the way."

"I believe you know Michael Russo."

"We've met, yes," Griswold said as if he'd just swallowed tree bark. "Whenever you trespass on the resort, police intrusion is never far behind."

"Nice to see you, too," I said.

"You've brought a member of the press with you, I see."

"Lighten up, Ward," Frank said. "They're my guests."

"A pity," Griswold said. He looked at Henri. "And who, I might ask, is this one?"

"Name's Henri LaCroix, if that's any business of yours."

Griswold shook his head. "Everything around here is my business." He looked at the dead man. "What happened to this one?" Griswold said with a dismissive gesture.

"I shot him," Henri said.

"Indeed."

"This is private property. Why don't all of you get out? Take the dead one with you."

"They can't do that Ward," Frank said. "You know that. The police will want to talk to them."

"They can damn well talk to them somewhere else." Griswold turned my way. "Mr. Russo, take your friend with the gun, and the other man over there and leave. Take the dead man with you. And the girl."

"The girl?" AJ said. "The girl?"

"Yes, you," Griswold said.

Henri went over to Griswold. "Shut up," he said. "Or I'll shoot you, too."

"What did you say your name was?"

"LaCroix. Need me to spell it?"

"I'll put you in jail for threatening me, Mister."

"Henri," I said, "it'd be my pleasure to represent you in court if you want to shoot him."

"You're hired," Henri said.

"Have fun, gentlemen," Griswold said, "but I can break both of you, should I choose to do so."

We heard sirens in the distance. They grew louder then went off. Moments later, an Emmet County patrol car pulled into the driveway followed by an ambulance and a Jeep driven by the kid from the gate-house.

Both patrol officers stepped out of the car but kept the open doors between them and us. They had their guns out.

Henri and I took a few steps in front of the others and held our jackets open.

"We both have handguns," I said.

The kid from the jeep pointed and said something to the officer.

"One of you Russo?"

"Me," I said.

"Take out your guns, very slowly, put them on the ground and step back," he said.

We did.

The officer nodded and a woman and a man got out of the ambulance and moved quickly to the body.

The two officers came up followed by the kid from the Jeep.

"Holy shit," the kid said and moved away from the body. "Guy dead?" he said.

"Yes," one of the EMTs said. Another siren grew louder.

The officer who'd done all the talking was tall, maybe thirty and a little heavy. He looked at me.

"Hal," the officer said. "Keep an eye on these people for a minute." He gestured at me. "Over here, Mr. Russo," he said and walked back towards the patrol car. I followed.

The siren was very loud, then it wasn't.

"I'm supposed to wait for the State detective to get here," he said. "But why don't you tell me who the dead man is and which one of you shot him."

Before I could say much worth listening to, a sedan pulled to the edge of the driveway and stopped. Captain Martin Fleener climbed out of the car. He didn't look happy.

37

Fleener walked slowly up to us.

"Officer," Fleener said. "What do we got?"

"Sir," the officer said. "One dead. Male. This one," he gestured at me, "was armed. And the tall man over there. In the tan jacket."

"LaCroix?"

"Don't know his name yet, sir. We just got here."

"Henri had a handgun, Marty," I said.

"Of course he did." Fleener went to his car and came back with a plastic cup.

"A little late at night for that, isn't it?" I said.

"Never investigate a crime scene you don't have coffee," he said. "Officer, lead the way."

We walked up the driveway to the others. Fleener looked at the people standing around the body. And at the body. He said hello to the other officer. Fleener pointed at the kid in baggy jeans and said, "Put cuffs on this one, Officer. Read him his rights and sit him in your car."

"Yes, sir."

"Arrest this one, too," Griswold said, stretching his arm full length, pointing at Henri.

Fleener turned his head. "What's your name, sir?"

"Griswold," he said indignantly, "Wardcliff Griswold. I'm president of Cherokee Point Resort Association."

Fleener nodded. "Right, right. I remember you."

"As well you should."

"Un-huh," Fleener said. "Why am I supposed to arrest this man?"

"He told me he shot the dead man."

"You shoot the dead man, Henri?"

"Yes."

"See and he threatened to shoot me, too. I demand you arrest him. Right now," Griswold said.

"Henri, you threaten to shoot Wardcliff here?"

"That's President Griswold to you, sir."

Fleener looked at Griswold and shook his head.

"Did you threaten President Wardcliff, Henri?"

"Yes."

"See," Griswold said. "Do you think I'd make that up? Now arrest him."

Another patrol car pulled to a stop near the other cars. An officer climbed out and walked up the driveway.

"Were you here when the shooting took place?" Fleener said to Griswold.

"No, I arrived later."

"Go home, Mr. Griswold," Fleener said. "We'll talk to you later."

"I will not leave until . . ."

"Go home now," Fleener said.

"I won't be told what to do on private property," Griswold said. "Not by you or anybody else. Is that clear?"

Fleener went over to Griswold, got in close, and said, "Go home, Griswold, or I might just let Henri shoot you. Am I clear?"

Henri grinned. "Be happy to help any way I can, Captain."

"That's enough," Griswold said. "I'll have your badge for this. You all heard him. You're witnesses."

All of us had a sudden interest in the stones on the driveway. No one said a word. Finally, at last, Griswold was quiet. He turned and walked back into the shadows.

Fleener tried to drink some coffee, but it was gone. He took off the plastic lid and looked inside, like that might help. It didn't.

"Okay, here's how it's gonna go," Fleener said. He looked at Frank and Ellen. "Is it all right if we use your kitchen or the living room? For preliminary interviews. We shouldn't be too long."

"Of course," Frank said. "We can make fresh coffee, too."

"That'd be nice," Fleener said staring at his empty cup one more time.

"Officer Caruso, isn't it?" Fleener said to the most recent arrival.

"Yes, sir," the man said. Like the others, he was young, fresh-faced but not as eager.

"Thanks for coming this late," Fleener said. "Why don't you follow Mr. Marshall and Ms. Paxton in the house and take their statements."

"Yes, sir," he said, "will do."

Fleener said to the other officers, "Stay here until the medical people have done their work then take your boy," he gestured at the man in the backseat of the patrol car, "to the station."

The officers nodded.

"Well, that leaves us, doesn't it," Fleener said to Henri, AJ and me. "Let's go inside and talk."

We started towards the back door when Fleener said, "Go on ahead. I got to call Don Hendricks. He won't be happy."

enri and I followed AJ into the house and through the kitchen. Frank had put on a fresh pot of coffee. Officer Caruso sat at the dining room table, so recently occupied by our more amiable group, and took notes as he talked with Frank and Ellen. We went to the living room, sat down and waited for Fleener.

"The Captain's not a happy man," Henri said. "Griswold didn't help any."

"No," I said. "That arrogant little prick's a pain in the ass."

"You two are missing the big picture," AJ said.

"Want to enlighten us, Ms. Reporter?"

"Cut the sarcasm, Russo," AJ said. "Fleener's pissed because he's got another shooting and this time a dead body." She shook her head.

I started to say something when Captain Fleener came into the living room and took an empty chair by the fireplace. He carried his coffee cup and a small plate with two sugar cookies on it. He put them on a round glass-topped table next to the chair. Fleener was dressed impeccably, as always. A two piece dark gray suit over a white shirt with a black and red checked tie. Even his black wingtips were polished. He'd probably been in his favorite chair, in a sweatshirt and sweatpants, talking with his wife, Helen, when the call came. But ever the professional, Captain Fleener was ready to work.

"Just got off with Don Hendricks," Fleener said. "He'd dozed off on the couch. Pissed about more gunplay."

AJ no doubt rolled her eyes, but I refused to look over. We sat quietly. Fleener took care of one cookie in two bites and followed it with a drink of coffee.

"Jesus, Henri," Fleener said. "Did you have to shoot the guy?"

"Only way, Captain."

"The only way?" Fleener said. "You learn that in Iraq?"

"Guy spins around puts a gun on me, I shoot," Henri said. "I learned that here at home."

"He's right, Marty," I said. "I'd done the same thing."

Fleener shook his head. "All right, all right," he said. He picked up the other cookie and took a bite. "Don said you can give formal statements tomorrow morning. Eight o'clock sharp. No excuses. Understand?"

I nodded and AJ said yes.

"Henri?"

"Eight o'clock. I'll be there."

Fleener finished the cookie and drank the last of his coffee.

"Now tell me what happened. From the top," he said. "You first, AJ. I trust your reporter's eyes," he gestured towards Henri and me, "a lot more than our gunslingers, here."

Henri didn't say anything. Me, either.

AJ told the story from the time we said goodbye to Frank and Ellen. She finished in a few minutes. Focused, detailed, and clear. Just like her reporting.

Fleener nodded. "Thank you, AJ," he said. "You two want to add anything?"

Henri shook his head.

"Yes," I said. "Henri did the right thing, Marty."

Fleener nodded. "I started my day with you," he said. "End with you, too. Make it worth my time. You owe me."

"These two kids aren't the men who shot Frank," I said.

"Took us only a few hours of legwork to figure that out," Fleener said. "Tell me something I don't know."

"But they are connected to the shooting," I said.

"That so?"

"It is," I said. "That night at Bernie's, one kid said 'Chicago' wanted me off the case. 'Chicago.'"

Fleener thought for a minute. "Chicago."

I nodded and gave him the highlights of Morgan and the Marshall brothers.

"You couldn't have told me this before?"

"Wasn't sure before?"

"But you're sure now?"

I nodded.

Fleener got up and went to the door to the dining room.

"Frank."

"Captain?"

"Russo's theory about a revenge killing. You believe it?"

"Enough that he's got me listening."

Fleener came back to his chair. He stared at the small plate with a few cookie crumbs on it.

"Why are you sure now?"

"A few more pieces have fallen into place," I said.

"Any of those pieces Joey DeMio?"

Sometimes I forget that Fleener's a smart cop. He's very good at what he does. When most people guess, they're guessing. His guesses are conclusions based on experience and homework.

"Could be," I said.

"Dump the bullshit, Russo," Fleener said. "You owe me information. Remember?"

"I remember."

"Well, then? Is DeMio part of this or not?"

"I asked Joey to check out Morgan. See if he ordered the hit on Frank."

"He confirm?"

"Yeah," I said, "but it was Phil Morgan, of course, not his dead father."

"Think DeMio approved the hit?"

I shrugged.

"Was he doing a favor for Morgan?"

"Don't know," I said. "Joey and Phil Morgan got business together. Not sure if that includes a hit."

"But you think Joey's connected to the hit."

"Not much happens in Chicago mafia land that he doesn't know about."

"Did Joey send the kids to beat you up?"

"No," I said. "Not his style. If he sent guys to beat me up, I'd be a helluva lot worse off than a black eye."

"You seem awful sure," Fleener said.

"That's what he told me."

Fleener rubbed his eyes with his fingers. He looked tired or frustrated or both.

"We got Morgan in Chicago. DeMio on Mackinac Island. Frank in Petoskey. Punks from Mac City. They're all connected somehow," Fleener said, "and we're still no closer to arresting the shooters."

"No, we're, not," I said.

"A few theories but no proof is all we got." Fleener picked up the plate and the cup and got out of his chair. "Time to go home," he said. "Helen's probably asleep on the couch."

We went to the kitchen. Officer Caruso had finished with Frank and Ellen who stood at the sink counter.

"It's late," I said to no one in particular.

"Tomorrow morning," Fleener said. "In the office." He put on his coat. "I'll move our cars out of the way so you can get your car out, Michael."

"No need," Frank said. "Just drive across the grass to the road."

"Won't President Griswold object?" Fleener said. He stopped at the door. "What if he calls the cops?"

39

I sat with AJ and Henri at a small table in the window at Roast & Toast. It was a little after seven. A steady rain came down. The sky was dark enough that the street lamps lit up. We drank coffee.

"Think it'll snow?" Henri said.

"Still too warm," I said.

"This is Northern Michigan in October, Michael."

I nodded. "True."

"I got other things on my mind, you two," AJ said.

"Like what?" I said.

"Like keeping your ass in one piece."

"Think she doesn't want your ass shot up, Michael."

I smiled. "Me, either."

"Would you clowns shut up for a minute," she said. "I'm trying to be serious."

"Okay," I said. "Can I get more coffee first?"

"Sure, if you get me some, too," AJ said. I took her mug. "Henri?"

"No, thanks, Michael."

I refilled our mugs and sat back down. AJ took a drink.

"I'm listening," I said.

"Me, too, AJ," Henri said. "Sorry."

"Two things," she said. "You've seen DeMio twice."

"So?"

"You visited Mackinac Island's famous bad guy, and each time two guys from Mac City came after you." She paused for a second. "You don't think he sent them after you?"

"No, I don't," I said. "DeMio told me he'd . . ."

"I know what he told you. You believe him?"

"Something like this, yes," I said. "He's got no reason to lie." I raised my mug, pointing it for emphasis. "The threat of serious bodily harm pads his reputation. Those kids don't help his reputation any."

"Not sure I think you're right, but I'll let it pass for now. Which brings me to the other thing," AJ said.

"And that is?"

"Kellerman. You didn't tell Fleener about Kellerman last night. Why not?"

"Nothing to tell," I said.

"You said yourself Kellerman's seemed connected to all the other players."

I shrugged. "Just an educated guess."

"That begs the question why you didn't tell Fleener," AJ said.

"What do I tell him, AJ?" I said. "We suspect this, we think that. We're pretty sure this lawyer's part of the hit on Frank, but we're not positive."

"He threatened you," she said. "That day in your office."

I shrugged.

"You gonna mention Kellerman when we give our statements?"

I looked at my watch. "Hey, we gotta go. It's five of. Don't want to piss off Fleener."

"He's already pissed off," Henri said smiling.

We got up and put on our coats. I zipped the collar of my parka up tight.

"Answer my question, Michael?"

"About Kellerman?"

"Yes, about Kellerman," AJ said. "Now I'm getting pissed off. Give me a straight answer."

"If I learn something new on the way to the station, sure, I'll mention Kellerman."

We went out the door and headed up Lake Street.

"On the way to the station," AJ said, sounding disgusted, to say the least. "A five minute walk."

"Un-huh," I said.

"You can be a real ass sometimes, you know that?"

40

AJ and I leaned against the wall in the hallway of the Bodzick building and waited for Henri. Our separate interviews took little more than an hour.

"Knew Henri'd take longer," I said.

"How you figure?" AJ said.

"Because it's Henri. They don't like him," I said. "Even though his story's the same as ours."

"Except he shot a guy, Michael," AJ said.

"There is that."

I shifted my body and leaned against the wall with the other shoulder. It didn't help. We'd gotten home late. Too much happened last night for an easy night's sleep. So here we were, first thing in the morning, going over the events of a man's death again.

"You tell them about Kellerman?"

I shook my head. "They didn't ask," I said.

"Of course they didn't ask," she said. "How are they going ask about a guy . . ."

"Michael, AJ."

We looked down the hallway. Henri came towards us, walking slower than he usually did.

"You look tired," AJ said.

Henri shrugged. "More annoyed than tired," he said. "They went over the same ground, again and again. They knew it was a good shoot, but they kept asking anyway."

"Our stories were the same," I said.

"Yeah, they know that," Henri said. "Cop dropped off a file a few minutes ago. Figured it was your statements. Went quicker after that."

We started down the hallway towards the Bay Street entrance.

"Mr. Russo?"

We stopped and turned around. A uniformed officer came our way.

"Mr. Russo," she said. "Mr. Hendricks would like to see you."

"His office?"

"Yes, sir," the officer said. "Just you, sir."

"Thank you," I said.

"Okay, I'll catch up later. Where you gonna be?"

"Back to my hotel," Henri said. "Need a shower."

"To work," AJ said, "but I'd rather take a nap."

I said good-bye and went through the double doors and down the hall to the office of Donald Hendricks, Emmet County Prosecutor.

"Sit down," Hendricks said. I took the metal chair in front his desk. He pointed to a manila folder next to the telephone. "Your interviews," he said. "I'll get LaCroix's in a few minutes."

"They'll be the same, Don."

He nodded. "I know that," he said. "Talked with the officers who took the call this morning. It was a good shoot."

"Okay, can I go now?"

"No," Hendricks said. He leaned forward, put his elbows on the desk, and pointed at me. "I told you over a year ago, LaCroix's trouble."

"Not for me, he's not," I said.

"He shoots a guy is trouble for us," Hendricks said, "for Petoskey, for the county."

He put aside the interview file and opened another folder.

"Kevin Gayles, twenty-two, from Pickford." Hendricks shuffled the sheets of paper. "Started Mackinaw City schools in the eighth grade. Doesn't say why he moved down from the UP. Parents didn't."

"Abuse at home?" I said.

"Doesn't say. Be a reason to move, though."

"Where'd he live?"

"With the family of Alfred Crosette, our newest guest next door. Both kids dropped out of high school before senior year. Lived together in the back part of a house in Oden. No trouble with the law except a DUI for Gayles. Doesn't say anything about work, but they paid the rent, usually in cash."

"Drug money?"

"Probably," Hendricks said and closed the file. "No matter. Kid oughta be alive."

"You said yourself, it was a good shoot."

"Not the point, damn it," he said.

"What is your point, Don?"

"That LaCroix shot him at all. That it happened here."

"But you said . . ."

"I know what I said. But if he weren't here to help you, Russo, maybe that kid'd be alive."

"Or maybe I'd have shot him."

Hendricks nodded, slowly. "Maybe." He sat back. The tirade must be over. For now. Hendricks had to be under a lot of pressure. Cops, too.

"You get me here to talk about Henri LaCroix?"

Hendricks shook his head. "No."

"Then what?" I said.

"Fleener's about to interview Mr. Alfred Crosette. Want you to come along."

"Okay, but I got a question first."

"Thought you might," he said.

"Why you so nice to me?" I said. "According to you, I'm screwing things up."

"Get off your high horse, Russo," he said. "Don't confuse nice, as you call it, with self-interest."

Hendricks got out of his chair. "Kid's dead 'cuz of you. You're not getting' out of here just yet."

"Before we go," I said. "Why is a Captain of the State Police interviewing a high school dropout?"

Hendricks shook his head.

"Well?"

"You're not the only one doesn't like coincidences, Russo. Couple of punks come at you, okay, they're lookin' for fun. No harm done, except for that shiner of yours." He came around the desk. "But the same punks, two times?" Hendricks shook his head. "Got to be a reason."

"Any ideas?"

Hendricks shook his head. "That's why Marty's gonna take a shot. If something's there, he'll find it."

41

"**K**id should be here in a minute, Marty," Hendricks said.

We were in the small room next door to the interview room. Don Hendricks sat in his usual chair, at the edge of the large mirrored window. Martin Fleener sat at the back of the room with a cup of coffee, his metal chair tipped back against the wall. I sat across from Hendricks, on the other side of a small beige metal table.

"In no hurry, Don," Fleener said and sipped his coffee. Captain Fleener's reputation in the interview room was well known and much respected. Given enough information to work with, he'd run the interview like the director of a play. Give him scraps of information, he'd find a way to learn more as the interview went along.

He looked every bit the professional he was. His night went on longer than mine, but you'd never know it by looking at him. Well dressed as always, I was the only one who knew he'd worn the same suit last night.

Fleener dropped his chair to the floor. He put his coffee on the table next to a manila folder. He tapped the folder.

"Not much here, Don," he said.

Hendricks nodded.

"Are we missing something? Or is there really nothing?"

"Don't know," Hendricks said. "What do you think?"

Fleener shrugged. "I'm with you, Don. Got to be a reason these kids'd go after our friend here," he nodded in my direction, "two times." Fleener drank some coffee. "Everything else is a guess." Fleener slid the file in my direction. "What do you think, Russo?"

"Don't know what to think," I said and opened the file. "Does seem odd."

The door opened in the interview room and in walked Alfred Crosette and a uniformed officer.

"Pick a chair, that side," the officer said, pointing at two dull green metal chairs on one side of a gray metal table. Crosette pulled out a chair and sat down facing the window. He looked up at the mirror.

"Think he's been in a room before?" I said.

"That or he's watched too much *NCIS*," Fleener said.

"You're up, Marty," Hendricks said.

Fleener got up slowly and I handed him the file. He took a last drink of coffee and tossed the cup in the wastebasket.

"Could be blood out of a turnip."

"Wouldn't be your first," Hendricks said and laughed as Fleener went out the door.

Crosette watched Fleener carefully when he entered the interview room. Fleener nodded and the officer went out.

"Good morning, Mr. Crosette," Fleener said.

Crosette didn't answer, but he kept his eyes on Fleener.

In a series of choreographed moves, Fleener put the folder on the table and took off his suit coat. He carefully hung it over the back of the chair next to his and sat down. He took out a pen and put it down next to the folder.

"I love watching that man work," Hendricks said. "Establish who's in charge."

"In control, you mean," I said.

Hendricks nodded. "Same routine every time, no matter who's in the chair. Remember when he had Joey DeMio in there last year?"

"Hard to forget," I said. Fleener questioned DeMio for almost two hours during the Abbott murder investigation.

"Played Joey like a violin," Hendricks said. "All the time Joey's high-priced lawyer sat there tellin' him to shut up."

"Joey ignored him," I said.

"Thought he was smarter than Marty."

"Lotta people made that mistake."

"Good morning, Mr. Crosette," Fleener said again.

Crosette nodded.

"How are you, this morning?"

"Okay," Crosette said. He was about six feet, maybe one seventy-five and with a thin face. He still wore baggy jeans and the same plaid flannel shirt as last night. He tugged awkwardly at the sleeves of the shirt and moved his chair back. He put his hands in his lap.

"Do you know why you're here?"

Crosette shrugged. "Didn't shoot nobody," he said.

Fleener ignored his comment. "Would you like a lawyer, Mr. Crosette?"

Crosette shrugged. "Didn't do nothing need a lawyer for," he said.

Fleener ignored that comment, too. "But do you want a lawyer? Yes or no?"

Crosette shrugged again and said, "No."

Fleener leaned in and opened the folder. He picked up his pen and tapped it, absent mindedly, a couple of times on the table as he quietly read or pretended to read the file.

"That part of the show?" I said.

"Yep," Hendricks said. "Makes some people think he's not prepared."

"Another mistake?"

Hendricks nodded. "Un-huh."

"Alfred Martin Crosette. Twenty-two years old."

"Twenty-three," Crosette said.

Fleener looked up and nodded. "Twenty-three. Born and raised in Mackinaw City. Mac City schools until you dropped out of high school junior year." Fleener looked up again. "Why'd you drop out, Alfred?"

"Bored, man," he said and smirked like it was a dumb question.

"Bored," Fleener said.

"That's right."

"Says here you worked summers at a t-shirt shop, two of 'em actually, and a fudge shop. That right?"

Crosette chuckled. "Not all at the same time, man," he said, chuckling again like it was another dumb question.

"Right," Fleener said. "Not at the same time, but you did work summers on Central Avenue?"

"Guess so, man," Crosette said. "You got my papers there."

Fleener looked up.

"When'd you move to Oden?"

Crosette shrugged. "Two years ago? Three?"

"Why'd you move to Oden?"

"Bored, man. I was bored."

"In Mackinaw City?"

"Yeah."

"You were bored in Mackinaw City?"

"Yeah, Mac City," Crosette said, impatient with such stupid questions.

"Ever live any place else? Besides Oden, I mean?"

Crosette shook his head. "No."

"No brothers or sisters?"

"Kev's like a brother," he said.

"The late Mr. Gayles," Fleener said. "How long did he live with your family?"

"Kev was shot," Crosette said, louder than he'd said anything else. "You arrest the guy shot Kev?"

Fleener let the question pass.

"I seen it," Crosette said, agitated, edgy. "I'm a witness, man." He pointed at himself. "I seen the dude shot Kev. He didn't have to do that."

"Guess he missed the part about ole Kev having a gun," I said.

"Happens a lot," Hendricks said. "Can't figure out why they're in the room in the first place since they did nothing wrong."

"Dude shoots Kev," Crosette said. "Kev's shot. I get busted. That's fucked up, man."

"See what I mean?" Hendricks said.

"Didn't do nothing, man," Crosette said, clearly more agitated. "The fuck I doin' here, man?"

"Mr. Crosette," Fleener said, "you were arrested because you and Mr. Gayles pulled a gun and threatened to shoot people with it."

"Didn't have no gun," Crosette said.

"Another distinction that escapes Alfred," Hendricks said.

"Mr. Crosette," Fleener said, "why did you and Mr. Gayles threaten Michael Russo last night?"

Crosette put his elbows on the table and stared at the mirror over Fleener's shoulder but said nothing.

"That's the second time you went after Mr. Russo," Fleener said. "Why?"

Crosette continued to stare at the mirror. Maybe he was simply staring into space.

"Mr. Crosette, why did you and Mr. Gayles attack Mr. Russo outside Bernie's Bar?"

"Didn't do that, man," he said.

"Yeah, you did," Fleener said. "You were identified, you and Mr. Gayles. You beat up Mr. Russo at Bernie's. Why did you do that?"

Crosette said nothing.

"Why'd you and Gayles threaten Michael Russo with a gun last night?"

Crosette pulled his arms off the table and put them in his lap. He looked at Fleener.

"I want a lawyer."

"So much for the interview," I said.

"Well, that was quick," Hendricks said. "Too bad, too. When Marty gets a guy agitated and off balance, it usually leads somewhere interesting."

Fleener closed the folder and sat back. "You were read your rights, Mr. Crosette. The county will provide a lawyer . . ."

"Got my own lawyer, man," Crosette said. "Got the number. I want my lawyer."

"The fuck's goin' on?" Hendricks said. "Since when does a high school dropout have his own lawyer?"

Hendricks leaned over and rapped on the glass. Crosette looked up. Fleener stood up slowly, picked up his jacket and the folder.

"The officer will come get you in a minute," Fleener said.

Crosette smirked, again. "Got time, man," he said. "Got plenty of time."

Fleener came in the door and threw the folder on the table. "Little prick's got a lawyer?" he said.

"We wondered about that ourselves," Hendricks said.

"Don't fucking believe this," Fleener said. "Thought I was moving him to a good spot, too. His own lawyer?"

Fleener put his suit coat on and slid the manila folder in front of Hendricks.

"This is your problem now," he said to Hendricks. "Might as well get back to catching real criminals. Call me, Don."

"Yeah," Hendricks said and looked over at me. "Get out of here, Russo."

I followed Fleener out the door. He went down the hall, and I headed for the Lake Street exit.

The air was colder than earlier this morning and the sky was a brilliant blue. The sun hung low over the bay, its usual place for late October. It should make for a nice Northern Michigan afternoon. Especially for a run. Gotta work that in.

I pulled out my iPhone and hit AJ's number. The number rang but her voicemail picked up. "Headed to Roast & Toast for a bowl of soup. Come over, if you can."

It's a good thing I left Hendricks when I did. I could live with not telling him about Kellerman. No need to offer information, but I wouldn't have lied. In the end, Hendricks didn't ask.

Wonder if AJ would appreciate the subtly of my distinction? Doubt it.

I stopped at McLean & Eakin to pick up my *New York Times* and went next door for soup.

Roast & Toast was less crowded than I expected. I left my coat and the newspaper at one of the small booths on the wall. I ladled pea soup into a bowl, got an iced tea and sat down. I opened the *Times* and spread it out on the table. A few moments with a hard copy of the *Times* was a vanishing luxury.

"Hello, darling," AJ said. She leaned over and gave me a kiss.

"Thanks for the kiss," I said.

AJ put down her coat. "Be right back." She went to the counter and returned with a latte.

I folded up my paper. "That all you gonna have?" I said and drank some iced tea.

"I don't have much time, Michael," she said and looked at her watch.

"Breaking news?"

"God, how I hate that phrase."

"So you've said. What's up?"

"I'm going down to Lansing with Maury," she said. "But he'll be in a meeting for another half hour." She looked at her watch again and sipped the latte.

"Interviewing another potential intern for *PPD Wired?*"

She shook her head. "Second interview," AJ said. She wiped a bit of cream from her upper lip.

"Is this the MSU woman who worked at the *St. Ignace News?*"

"Yeah," AJ said. "If it goes well, Maury'll offer the job. I like her. Hope it works out."

"Well," I said, "good luck."

"Yeah, thanks. How'd your meeting with Hendricks go?"

"Wasn't a meeting exactly," I said. I told her what happened.

"You had an opportunity to tell him about Kellerman, but you didn't do it."

I shook my head as I ate a last spoonful of pea soup and pushed the bowl aside.

"Well, Michael, I've had my say on the subject. I'll leave it at that."

"You annoyed?"

AJ shrugged.

"What time will you get back from MSU?"

"Depends on what time we finish," she said. "If I have my way, we'll go to Dusty's for dinner before we leave."

"I get hungry just thinking about it," I said. "We should go down, stay a night or two and do that ourselves."

"Yes," she said, "we should. Maybe before Christmas." She looked at her watch again. "Got to go, Michael," she said. "Call you when I get back."

"Want to come to my place?"

She shook her head. "Not sure what time I'll get home. I'll be tired. How about a rain check for tomorrow night?" she said. "You can fix dinner and I'll do some wonderfully sleazy things to your body for desert. How's that sound?"

"Sounds wonderfully sleazy," I said. "Want to give me a hint?"

"Not now, darling," she said with a big smile. "I can't be late."

We kissed and AJ waved as she went out the door.

I took the dishes to the counter, picked up my newspaper and coat and went to the office.

Sandy was gone, but she left a note, and a welcome note it was. No messages, no problems, no gunslingers looking to put a bullet in my hide. I'll catch up on a few case files and go home. I'll run four or five miles through Bay View, make some pasta for dinner and watch a movie.

42

I sat quietly, drinking coffee, reading the *New York Times*, and eating a pecan roll. I was in no particular hurry this morning. AJ was back from Lansing happy about her new assistant, I had no appointments, and I caught up on paperwork yesterday. My phone buzzed on the table. The caller ID was blocked, but only a few people have my number. I swiped the screen and answered the call.

"Russo, where are you?"

"Marty?"

"Yeah," he said, "where are you?"

"Julienne Tomatoes. Why?"

"Pick you up in two minutes. Be outside."

I stuffed two more bites of pecan roll in my mouth and followed it with coffee. I grabbed my coat and brief bag and headed outside. A light rain came down at a tough angle pushed by a heavy wind. I zipped up tight and waited in the shelter of the doorway.

Fleener's black sedan came up Howard from Mitchell too fast for the street and hit the brakes. He laid on the horn until he saw me start across the street.

"Marty," I said, trying to close the car door as he took off. He pulled a hard left at Michigan Street without bothering to stop for the sign, then over to Mitchell and away from downtown.

"We seem to be in a hurry."

"Gotta a stiff," Fleener said. "Want you to see him."

"Okay."

Fleener went left at Division, passed two cars down the hill and took U.S. 31 north. He lowered the window, slapped a light on the roof, and hit the siren. Cars scattered however they could. Fleener moved carefully and quickly around them. Once 31 turned into two lanes, he moved faster, not waiting for cars to get out of the way.

"Where we going?"

"Crooked Lake."

The lake ran parallel to U.S. 31 a couple of miles north of town. It's a large, craggy shaped lake lined with cottages, some from the 1920s, some newly built where old places once stood. At the North Conway Road, Fleener killed the siren and hit the brakes. He pulled into a small parking lot at the boat launch and stopped. Cop cars everywhere and an ambulance. As we climbed out of the car, I saw Don Hendricks standing over a body bag. He didn't look happy. Fleener and I walked over.

"Don," I said.

"Russo," he said. "Harry, open the top of the bag, will you."

One of the EMTs, a man in his twenties, unzipped the bag.

"Take a look."

I moved closer.

"Recognize him?"

I nodded. "Guy named Kellerman," I said. "Forgot the first name."

"James," Fleener said.

"Right, James," I said. "What killed him?"

"Two in the chest," Hendricks said. "A nine mill, probably. We'll know more after the ballistics report."

"He shot here?"

"Doubt it," Hendricks said. "Pretty sure the body was dumped here overnight."

Hendricks turned to me, the first time since I arrived that he'd looked at anything but the body.

"Guy had your card in his wallet, Russo. Why?" He didn't wait for an answer. "We got three people shot," he said. "Two of 'em dead, and you're connected to all three. How come?"

"Not sure I'm connected, Don," I said.

"Bullshit," he said. "Frank Marshall's your friend." Hendricks was angry. "LaCroix put one in the chest of the guy beat you up." He jabbed his hand at the body bag. "Now Kellerman here's got your card."

"I still don't see . . ."

"You know Kellerman's a lawyer?"

"Yeah," I said.

"You know that when Fleener interviewed Alfred Crosette?"

"Where you going with this, Don?" I said.

"When Crosette said he wanted his own lawyer yesterday, you know it was Kellerman?"

"Maybe," I said.

"Maybe?" Hendricks shook his head. "You're fuckin' with me, Russo. You and LaCroix."

Hendricks put his hands on his hips and looked out over Crooked Lake. He was quiet for a minute.

"Where is LaCroix?"

"Not sure," I said.

Hendricks turned and glared at me.

"Bullshit," he said. "Get your goddamn phone out. Call LaCroix. You're holding out on me, Russo. You made a deal for information. Time we got it."

Hendricks' voice grew louder the angrier he got. I kept quiet. Nothing I said at this point would help.

"Be in my office, both of you," he pulled back his coat sleeve and looked at his watch, "in two hours. Understand? This isn't a request, god-damn it. Be there. I'll send the fucking sheriff you don't show up. I'll put you in handcuffs and I'll put your ass in jail."

I started to say something, but Hendricks shot back, "Don't pull legal shit on me. I'll throw you in the drunk tank, you're not there. Under-stand?"

I nodded. "Yeah."

"You're in this," Hendricks said. "Both of you. Not sure how, but you're in it."

43

got a ride back to town in one of the patrol cars. The officers dropped me at my apartment. I went upstairs and called Sandy at the office.

"That's all you're going to tell me?" she said. "That I can quit looking for Kellerman 'cuz he's floating in Crooked Lake?"

"He's not in the lake, Sandy," I said. "His body was found at the boat launch."

"I get it, Michael," she said. "I want to know what's going on."

"Me, too," I said. "But that's all I got right now."

Sandy sighed loudly. "You get hold of Henri?"

"Un-huh," I said. "Meeting him in a few minutes."

"Try not to piss off Hendricks any more, will you."

"Try my best," I said. "Don't want to land in jail."

"I'll find you a good lawyer, boss," Sandy said and hung up.

I left my apartment. The rain had eased up, but the wind hadn't let up at all. I went across the parking lot and into the lobby of the Perry Hotel. Henri stood at the window looking down the street towards the Bodzick Building.

"You staring at the Sheriff's office?" I said as I walked up to the window.

Henri shook his head. "Not really," he said. "You know, Michael, I can't figure out if we know more than we think we know but don't have the pieces in place," he turned towards me, "or we just don't have it."

I shrugged. "Not sure I can help much," I said. "We've played enough you'd think we'd have it."

"But we don't," Henri said. "Now Kellerman gets himself dead. Any idea who did it?"

"No," I said, "but since nobody's found our two shooters, they get my vote."

"I'm not sure about that," Henri said.

"Me either."

"Know one thing though."

"And that is?"

"We gotta give Hendricks something," Henri said. "No ducking him this time. We'd better agree on what to say."

"Yeah," I said. "Besides, I made a deal with Marty."

"Yes, you did," Henri said. "But it's your call."

"You have a say in this," I said. "Hendricks wants to beat on your ass, too."

"They'll have to get in line," Henri said, smiling. "You decide how much we tell them and I'm in."

I put my hands in my pockets and looked out the window. I stood there and just stared. I thought it might help. It didn't. "Let's play it by ear," I said.

"Not much of a plan," Henri said.

I shrugged. "Let's go," I said. "Don't want to keep a pissed off man waiting."

We left the Perry. The rain had returned blown by the wind. I tugged at my coat. We went across Bay Street and into the County building. Hendricks' door was open when we got there. I knocked on the doorjamb anyway.

"Come on in," a voice said. It was Martin Fleener. He sat in his usual chair, on the wall, under the County map. "Nice of you gents to be on time," he said. "Don'll be back in a minute."

Two gray metal chairs, no doubt for us, were in front of Hendricks' desk. We sat down and didn't wait long.

Hendricks came through the door and put his large, rumpled frame behind the desk.

"Mr. LaCroix, Mr. Russo," he said. He was all business. When he used our first names, or a string of invectives, the conversation would be easy, the atmosphere relaxed. But when Donald Hendricks was all business, well, the time for fucking around was over. His sleeves rolled up, Hendricks leaned forward, elbows on the desk.

"Marty and I got back to town a while ago," he said. "Got some coffee and sat in my car."

"In your car?" I said. "Lotta good coffee shops for that, Don."

He ignored me. "We needed to figure out what to do with you two," he said. "Didn't want to be interrupted."

He heard me after all.

"You can thank the Captain here," Hendricks nodded in Fleener's direction. "Despite my better judgment, he convinced me to give you one chance to quit fucking around and explain yourselves. I suggest you take it."

"One chance?" I said.

"To stop holding out on us," Hendricks said. "To tell us what you know, what you've found out since the night Frank Marshall was shot."

Hendricks slowly jabbed his hand in the air and pointed a finger at me.

"If I get so much as a twitch in my forehead that you're still fucking around. Well, let's just say I won't listen to Marty . . . see how you like jail."

"What you got's not jail," Henri said.

"Don't temp me, LaCroix."

"You gonna threaten me, better be real."

"Gentlemen, please," Fleener said. "Henri, cool down. We're all a little tight."

Hendricks leaned back in his chair. Now that he'd gotten that off his chest, we could get on with business.

"Two things straight off," he said. "Marty."

"First, we have not found the shooters," Fleener said. "Developed a few new leads," Fleener shook his head, "but they're not promising. Just so you know."

"Which brings us to Mr. Kellerman," Hendricks said.

"Got the medical report yet?" I said.

Hendricks shook his head. "I don't expect any surprises." He paused for a moment. Perhaps for effect.

"So, Mr. Russo, tell me about you and Mr. Kellerman."

"Don't know that much about the man," I said. "From Detroit. Not sure he has an office or where it is."

"Did you know he was Yale Law?" Hendricks said. "Editor of the Law Review?"

I shook my head. Yale? Why was this guy messing with high school dropouts?

"How'd you first meet?" Hendricks said.

I told them about Kellerman's visit to my office, about his property in Northern Michigan, and my about my suspicion of a link with Kevin Gayles and Alfred Crosette.

"A guy threatened you when you got nosey about the Marshall shooting, but it wasn't worth mentioning to us? We're trying to find the shooters, too, you know."

"Don," Fleener said.

Hendricks waved Fleener off. "See if I heard you right. Kellerman threatened you, mentioned Chicago. Two guys beat you up. They say something about Chicago." Hendricks rubbed his forehead with both hands. "A Yale lawyer represents two dropouts? I don't get it."

I shrugged. "Don't get it either, Don," I said.

"Let's not forget," Hendricks said, "about our Chicago hood up on Mackinac Island. I doubt he spends much time watching the horses go by. Did you ever think DeMio might be involved?" It was a rhetorical question. "Of course you thought of that," he said.

I nodded. "We thought of that, yes," I said.

"You know how DeMio's involved?" Fleener said.

"If he's involved."

"You said yourself not much happens DeMio doesn't know about. Let's assume he's involved. For what reason? What's he get out of killing Frank Marshall or threatening you?"

"Been wondering that myself," I said.

Fleener cocked his head.

"What?" he said. "You're thinking something. What is it, Russo?"

"Just a guess, you understand," I said.

"Okay."

"Let's say DeMio's running Kellerman. Might explain why our two kids have a Yale lawyer on retainer."

"DeMio's paying the tab?" Hendricks said.

"You think the kids got that kind of money?" I said.

"No, it's not the kids," Fleener said. "Certainly not Alfred Crosette."

"Be nice we could have questioned Mr. Kellerman," Hendricks said. "You come to us sooner we might've gotten a chance to do that. Cowboys. You think you're fucking John Wayne."

I ignored the jab. "Henri and I couldn't find him and we tried. Man was on the move all the time. Detroit, Traverse, here."

"Cops might've done better," Fleener said.

"Better?" I shrugged. "Guy knew how to fly under the radar."

"You got anything to add, Mr. LaCroix?"

Henri shook his head. "Nothing to add."

"How about the hired guns," Hendricks said. "You gentlemen tell me anything about them I don't know?"

Henri shook his head.

"Haven't found them," I said.

"Am I supposed to believe you, Mr. Russo?" Hendricks said.

"Don't care you do or not, Don," I said.

"Give me just one reason I should believe you."

I sat back in my chair, looked over at Fleener then back at Hendricks.

"If I found them, they'd be dead." I took in air and let it out slowly.

"If he didn't kill 'em," Henri said, jabbing a thumb at me hitchhiker style, "I'd have killed them."

Hendricks shrugged. "Cowboys," he said. It came out slow and easy. There was no tension in it. He sat back in his chair and rubbed his eyes.

"No more shooting," he said without irritation. "That clear, Henri?"

"It is."

"Michael, clear?"

He was back to first names. The question was asked without an edge.

"Yes, Don," I said.

"You got anything, Marty?" Hendricks said.

"All set for now, Don."

"Well, gentlemen," Hendricks said, "where do we go from here?"

"Find the shooters, Don," I said. "That's all that matters. Been that way from the start."

"We can't fight each other, Michael," Fleener said. "All that got us was a dead Kellerman." He got off his chair and went to the window near Hendricks' desk. He turned around and sat on the window ledge. "It's my job to arrest these guys for attempted murder. If they get dead in the process, so be it. But we gotta find 'em to arrest 'em."

"You got any idea who killed Kellerman?" Henri said.

"Could have been a random shooting," Fleener said.

"A random shooting and the body gets dumped at Crooked Lake?" I said. "You really believe that?"

"No," Fleener said, shaking his head.

"Who then?" Henri said.

"Best guess?" Hendricks said. "The same guys we're looking for."

"Motive?" I said.

Hendricks shook his head. "No idea."

"But that's your best guess?"

"It is," he said.

"So you really aren't any better off than the night Frank got shot?" I'd lost my angry edge, too. It didn't seem helpful anymore. "I just need to know, Don."

Hendricks looked down at his desk. Fleener got off the ledge and sat back down. They weren't eager to answer the question, but they weren't hostile to it either.

"No," Hendricks said, "we're not."

We were quiet. I shifted in my chair, trying to make it more comfortable.

"Well, it's been a long two days," I said. "Are we done?"

"Yeah," Hendricks said.

I got off the chair about the same time Henri did.

"Stay in touch," Hendricks said.

We said good-bye and went for the Lake Street exit.

Outside nothing had changed especially the rain. Still blown by the wind. I tugged on my collar.

We walked towards my office.

Henri zipped his coat.

"Your comment about jail," I said. "That about Iraq?"

"I don't like to be threatened," Henri said. "No teeth in that threat. Cell in Petoskey isn't jail. Mosul is jail. The hell of Karkuk is jail."

We walked along, hands in pockets, collars up against the rain and wind. Henri was quiet for a time.

"You know, I almost feel sorry for those guys," he said.

"Yeah?"

"We're no better off at finding the shooters, Michael, but we don't have the pressure they do."

"No City Council hounding us," I said.

"That's right," Henri said.

We waited for the light to change at Howard.

"Where you going?" I said.

"Hotel," Henri said. "Need a shower and a nap. I have plans for tonight."

"A little romance?"

"Of course," Henri said. "And a good dinner. How about you?"

"Check in with Sandy," I said. "Probably meet AJ after that."

"You come up with any ideas about the shooters, you let me know."

"You'll be the first one I call," I said.

44

"May I have more wine, darling?" AJ said.

We sat in her living room. While she took a shower, I built a fire that had just started to put heat in the room. I unwrapped a block of Manchego cheese, took a smaller piece of Swiss and put them on a plate with a few crackers. I opened bottle of Newton Chardonnay.

AJ was on the couch next to me wrapped in a huge white terry cloth robe with two big pockets. It gapped in front when she leaned forward to pick up a piece of cheese. I noticed. Her black hair hung in short, loose curls, still glistening from the shower. She drank the Chardonnay. I sipped an Oban, neat.

"Why of course, my sweet," I said, "anything your little heart desires." I took a paper napkin, shook it out, put it over my forearm with a flourish, took the bottle from the coffee table, and poured wine in her glass.

She sipped some wine. "My little heart, as you put it, darling, desires two things."

"Anything at all, my love."

She put down her glass and turned towards me. "First, cut the hammy stage actor routine. You're lousy at it."

"That bad?" I said.

"Un-huh," AJ said, "that bad."

"I kinda liked it myself," I said.

"If you don't cut it out, the second thing might get axed from the list."

"What would that be?" I said.

"I've seen you looking at my chest, darling," she said. "You're not the least bit subtle."

"Didn't want to be subtle," I said, smiling.

"Me either," she said and opened the front of her robe.

I stared and smiled again.

AJ pulled her robe closed and tugged on the terry belt. "Making love with you is the second thing," she said. "But I might put on my sweats you don't stop with the acting."

"Consider it done," I said.

AJ smiled. "Thought that might work." She opened a small but enticing gap in the front of the robe. "Finish your scotch," she said and picked up her glass. "We're in no hurry."

I ate some cheese without a cracker and swirled the Oban in my glass.

"That the scotch I got for your birthday?"

I nodded. "A wonderful choice," I said. "Thank you."

"You're welcome," she said and raised her glass towards mine.

"Do you think Hendricks was really angry at you and Henri," AJ said, "or just yanking your chain?"

"Sandy asked me that, too," I said. "Fact is, I'm not sure."

"I told you at Frank's house that Hendricks was angry at a second shooting. Now he's got another body." She put some cheese and a cracker on the napkin in her lap. "Maybe he's just scared he can't get a handle on this thing."

"And he thinks Henri and I are in the way."

"You are in the way, darling," she said and raised her glass.

I took a last drink when I heard a familiar buzz coming from the end table next to the couch. It buzzed again.

"See who it is," AJ said.

"You sure?"

She nodded and I reached for my phone.

"It's Pam Wiecek," I said and swiped the screen. I tapped speaker and set it on the coffee table.

"Pam," I said, "what's up?"

"Mr. Russo," she said, "how are you?" Her voice sounded agitated. I looked at AJ. She caught it, too.

"What is it, Pam?"

"Mr. Russo," she said. "I owe you a lot. You know, for Laurie."

"You paid your bill," I said, trying to be helpful.

"No, no," she said. "I'm in the women's room."

"Un-huh."

"At work."

"Okay." I glanced at AJ. She shrugged.

"Two guys," she said, "at the bar. One's got a gun. I heard your name."

AJ sat forward and closed her robe up tight.

"Recognize them, Pam?"

"They're not from around here," she said. "Tried to listen after that."

"What did they say?"

"Only got a few words," she said. "Can't stay in here, Mr. Russo. Bar's busy tonight."

"What else did they say, Pam?"

"Something about a passport. Look I gotta go."

"Can you keep them there?"

"They got menus," she said. "Food'll take a while if they order."

"I'm on my way, Pam. Do your best." I clicked off my iPhone. I slipped on my shoes, got up and went to the back door. My gun hung with my heavy parka.

"Michael," AJ said.

I stopped and looked back.

"Shouldn't you call the Mac City cops?"

"And tell 'em what? Don't know if it's the right guys. By the time I answer questions, they'll be gone."

I clipped the holster to my belt and zipped up my coat.

"Call Henri," I said. "Tell him what happened. Don't care where he is, tell him to get to Mac City fast."

"Michael," she said and hesitated. She came towards me. "Watch yourself, will you? And drive carefully." She gave me a light kiss.

"I love you," I said. "Call Henri."

"Lots of deer this time of night," I heard her say as I went out the door. The air was crisp, clear and getting colder each night.

I got in the BMW and started the motor. I opened the console, took out the radar detector and stuck it to the windshield. It beeped four times when I turned it on.

I went over to Mitchell, took it north to Division and down the hill to U.S. 31.

Pam Wiecek said two men were in the bar. One had a gun and my name. Not much to go on, but it's something.

I watched my speed on 31 until I got north of the BP station. I gradually moved faster, wanting to get a feel for the traffic. It was light.

Passports. Two men, a gun and something about passports? I still don't believe in coincidences. It's gotta be them. They know my name? Gotta be the shooters. Nothing else made sense.

North of Alanson, I saw very few cars. I left the Xenons on bright. They lit up the road and the shoulders. I moved very quickly slowing up only at Pellston and Levering.

My phone rang on the other seat. I picked it up, punched the speaker and dropped it back on the seat.

"Where are you?" Henri said.

"Thirty-one, just short of I-75."

"Moving?" he said.

"About 125," I said. "Where are you?"

"Levering," Henri said. "Think it's them?"

"Hell if I know."

"Think they're still there?"

"Don't know that either."

"Wait for me," he said. "These guys are pros, remember. Have a beer. Watch 'em."

"A beer?"

"Don't do anything stupid. They leave, tail 'em. I'll find you."

"Almost to the exit at Audie's," I said. "Get that truck of yours moving."

Henri laughed and the call went dead.

45

I wanted the last exit before crossing the Mackinac Bridge.

I hit the brakes hard, downshifted once then again, and turned off I-75 at Jamet Street. That put me right next to Audie's. Couldn't have been more than a half dozen cars in front of the restaurant. I parked next to an old beat up red Chevy. A '63 Impala.

I picked up my iPhone and put into the left jacket pocket. I took my gun out and chambered one round. I slipped it into the other jacket pocket.

Nobody on the street. I got out of the car and went up the sidewalk to the front door.

Audie's Restaurant has been around more than fifty years, as long as the Mackinac Bridge has carried traffic across the Straits. AJ and I often stopped for breakfast or for a quiet dinner on our way to the Michigan's Upper Peninsula. Tonight I was headed for the bar next to the dining room and food was not on my mind.

I went in the front door and eased my way around a decorative room divider and into the bar. It was almost empty. One man in a dark green MSU sweatshirt sat at the bar watching the Tigers-Yankees playoff game. A middle-aged couple sat at a table on the other side of the room. They watched only each other. I took a seat at the end of the bar to get a clear view of the room.

Pam Wiecek came around the corner, put a bowl of soup down in front of the baseball fan and refilled his soft drink. She saw me and smiled.

"Mr. Russo," she said. "Hello."

"The men gone, Pam?"

She nodded. "Yeah. Didn't order food. Finished their drinks and left."

I took my hand out of my jacket pocket and relaxed.

"What can I get you, Mr. Russo?"

"Black coffee would be great, Pam." She went to the other end of the bar and came back with a steaming cup of coffee and a glass of water.

"Sorry I couldn't keep 'em here longer," she said.

"Nothing you could do," I said. I took off my coat and put it over the back of the chair.

The door opened and Henri walked in. He stopped to look over the room just as I had done. He saw me and I nodded. He came around the divider.

"Henri, this is Pam Wiecek."

"Pleased to meet you," he said and reached out his hand.

"Thanks," Pam said and they shook hands. "Get you something?"

"Iced tea," he said and sat down.

She nodded and went down the bar.

"Anything?"

"Gone when I got here," I said. "Haven't talked with Pam yet."

"Well, let's do that," he said.

She put a tall glass in front of Henri.

"Can you talk, okay?" I said.

She nodded. "Yeah. It's cleared out pretty good," she said and looked over the room.

"How long they been gone?"

"Fifteen minutes, twenty maybe."

"You said they weren't from here."

"Yeah," she said. "I mean no, not from here."

"How could you tell?"

"You work a bar, you can tell," she said. "Clothes, how they talk, the way they treat us."

"Describe them," Henri said.

"Well, a Mexican and a black," she said. "Pretty odd around here."

"How'd you know one was from Mexico?" I said.

She shrugged. "Looked Mexican, you know."

"Accent? Appearance?"

Pam shook her head. "No accent." She thought for a minute. "Maybe not Mexico, exactly," she said. "But dark skin and real thick black hair. Maybe Spanish. I dunno. Big guy, kinda chubby."

"The other guy?" Henri said. "The black man?"

"He was shorter, skinny." Pam refilled my coffee. "A real nervous type, you know."

"Light skin or dark?" I said.

"Light, I guess." She thought for a minute. "Yeah, light. Short hair, too."

"Why'd you think he was nervous?" Henri said.

"Couldn't sit still," Pam said. "Fidgety. Watched the room all the time." We heard the door open. Henri looked up.

Two women in their thirties, casually dressed in jeans and crewneck sweaters and obviously having a good time, took a table away from the bar, near the other couple.

Henri watched them carefully. "There're okay," he said.

"Back in a second," Pam said. She took menus to the women and got a drink order. When she finished, she came back to us.

"On the phone, you told me one of the men had a gun and mentioned my name."

She nodded. "The Mexican, yeah," she said. "The gun was here," she pointed at her left arm, "under his coat."

"Shoulder holster?"

"Yeah," she said.

"And passports," I said. "What about passports?"

Pam leaned forward, arms out stretched, hands on the edge of her side of the bar.

"I only caught words, here and there. Know what I mean?"

"Sure," I said. "What else?"

"We were really busy, you know. It's not like I could stand there and listen to every word or anything."

"We understand," Henri said in a soft, affirming voice. "You did what you could."

"I did," she said, "really, I did."

"What about the passports?" I said.

She stood up and crossed her arms over her chest. "Well, I don't think they had 'em."

I started to ask the obvious question when one of the two women said from their table, "Miss. We'd like to order."

"Be right back," Pam said and walked away.

"We're wasting time if those guys are still in town," Henri said.

"Where do we look?" I said. "Could be anywhere."

Henri shrugged. "I'm just saying."

When Pam came back, I said, "Why do you think they didn't have passports?"

"Who talks about a passport you already got one?"

"Good point," I said, smiling.

"Thing is, who needs a passport for Pellston?"

"Pellston?" Henri said. "They talk about Pellston?"

She nodded. "Heard it a couple of times," she said. "How Pellston wouldn't take long. Like that." Pellston, twenty minutes south of Mackinaw City, had a commuter airport feeding Detroit.

Pam wiped her hands on a towel. "Got a food order coming up. More coffee, Mr. Russo?"

"No, thanks," I said.

When Pam went away, I said to Henri, "But you need a passport to get out of the country."

"Yes, you do," Henri said. "Only one airline at Pellston."

"Delta," I said. "To Detroit."

"Something to go on," Henri said.

"What's not far from Pellston?" I said.

"Pellston's very far from everything," Henri said.

"You know what I mean," I said.

"Un-huh," Henri said. "Could be their hideout, I suppose."

"Yes," I said, "it could."

"Two gunmen at a hideout," Henri said. "Got a movie for that one?"

"Got a whole list of 'em," I said. "Where would you like me to start?"

"How 'bout we start by getting out of here," Henri said.

"Okay. I'll call AJ. Tell her we're on our way. She was worried I'd do something stupid if the shooters were here."

"She's not the only one," Henri said.

I looked at Henri and shook my head.

I dropped a ten on the bar and we waved goodnight to Pam.

The moon lit up the street and it was colder. But the wind was gone. We stopped next to my car.

"On the way up here," I said, "I figured something out." I leaned back against the car and crossed my arms. The lights of the Mackinac Bridge gleamed in the crisp night air. Workers for the Bridge Authority would soon change all the lights to red and green, yellow and blue for Christmas.

Henri leaned on the old red Impala. "What did you figure out?"

"I wanted those guys to be here," I said. "I wanted the gunmen who tried to kill Frank."

"Yes?" Henri said.

"I wanted them to come at me," I said. I looked at Henri. I saw it in his eyes. In the light of the moon, in the soft glow of the Audie's sign, I saw it in his eyes.

"I thought I just wanted to find them."

"But that wasn't enough, was it?" Henri said.

I shook my head. "I wanted to kill them myself."

"Now you know," he said.

I shrugged and looked up at the bridge.

"Lots of people scream they're gonna kill somebody, Michael. In anger, or hate or an alcoholic rage."

"That isn't me, Henri."

"No, it isn't. A few people have a clear head about killing. You had a chance to get the men who tried to kill your closest friend. You were ready for it, Michael. More important, you decided to be ready for it."

"That's not the world I've live in, Henri."

"It is now, Michael," he said. "It is now."

46

"That's all Pam told you?" AJ said. "They might have passports and they talked about Pellston. That's it?"

We were in AJ's living room. She'd traded the white robe for a pair of black running pants and a faded green sweatshirt with blotches white paint here and there. She'd added a couple of logs to the fire, and opened a bottle of wine. Henri sat on the floor near the fireplace. AJ and I were on the couch. I put my feet on the coffee table and held a glass of wine in my lap.

"Well, her brief description of the men, too," Henri said.

"Hispanic and African-American," AJ said.

"Not the way she said it, but yeah."

"Does that help?" AJ said.

"A little," I said. "It's how Pam knew they weren't locals."

AJ sipped some wine and thought for a minute. "I think it adds up," she said. "I think you got a real lead."

"That's wishful thinking," Henri said.

"No, it's not," she said. "It's the reporter in me. There's something there. I can smell it. We haven't found it yet, that's all."

"Can Lois Lane be more specific?" I said.

"Pick a better role model and I'll try."

"Hildy Johnson?"

"That is better," AJ said. "I always liked Rosalind Russell."

"Then I'm Cary Grant," I said.

"Now that's wishful thinking, darling," she said, sarcastically.

"Could you two cut the movie banter and get back to passports and Pellston?"

I nodded, sheepishly. So did AJ.

AJ took a drink of wine. "All right," she said. "Michael, there's shaved turkey, some tomatoes and lettuce. Sourdough bread's in the basket. Make us sandwiches."

"That's your idea of being more specific?" I said.

"Shut up," she said and pointed to the kitchen. "Now. We're gonna be here awhile."

She poured more wine in her glass. "Henri?"

Henri shook his head. "Might take a sandwich though."

"Okay," AJ said. "From the top. Let's see what we got."

Two turkey sandwiches later, for Henri and me, we sat quietly, thinking about what to do next. AJ, who skipped a sandwich but nibbled on potato chips, said, "I have an idea."

We looked up.

"Well?" I said.

She ran both hands through her hair, leaned forward and put her elbows on her knees. "Let's assume the following," she said, "for the sake of argument. First, the two men at Audie's are, in fact, the assassins. Second, they need passports with bogus names because they're leaving the country, and, three, they're flying out of Pellston to do it."

"Lot of assumptions," I said.

"Shut up, Michael," Henri said. "Let her talk."

AJ smiled at Henri.

"Passports and plane tickets. There's a way to track that," she said. "Homeland Security's got a no-fly list. The State Department checks for fraudulent passports all the time. The NSA spies on people every day, right? We should be able to find out if the pieces go together. Just don't know how to do it, that's all."

"Too bad we can't call the NSA and ask for a drone or something," Henri said. He sounded serious.

"Hildy Johnson would have known what to do," AJ said sounding frustrated.

"Easy to know what to do on the silver screen, AJ," Henri said.

She nodded. "Doesn't make me feel any better, but thanks." She thought for a minute. "But there is someone we can call. And not Cary Grant or Rosalind Russell."

"Good thing," Henri said. "Been a long day. Get on with it."

"A real reporter. Lenny Stern."

"The old guy works for the paper?" Henri said.

AJ nodded. "He knows people in Chicago."

"Good for him," Henri said. "How's that help us?"

"Passport Agency's got a branch in Chicago," I said. "State Department, too."

"You think Stern's got contacts like that?"

"Lenny's got contacts everywhere," AJ said.

"Would he help?" Henri said.

"One way to find out," I said. I looked at my wrist with no watch. "What time is it?"

"Little after twelve," Henri said. "Why?"

"I'll show you why. Hand me my phone," I said to AJ. "It's on the side table."

She picked up the iPhone and gave it to me.

I hit contacts and punched Lenny Stern's number.

"Don't know if he'll answer this late," I said, "but what the hell."

I waited. "Got his voicemail," I said, not happily. When the message finished, I said, "Lenny. It's Michael Russo. Sorry it's late. Pick up, will you. It's about the Frank Marshall shooting. Could be a great story in it. Call me now. Please."

"Think he'll get it?" Henri said.

"Don't know," I said. "Wait and see, I guess."

We didn't have to wait long. The iPhone buzzed on the coffee table. No caller ID on the screen. It had to be him.

"Lenny?" I said. "Sorry. Thanks for calling back."

"Better be a good story, Michael," Stern said. "I'm kinda tied up at the moment. If you know what I mean?"

I ignored him and pressed on.

"AJ says you got good contacts in Chicago."

"Of course I do. What do you want?"

"That include the Passport Agency?"

Silence.

"Maybe," he said. "Why?"

"How about the State Department office?"

"This better make a good story because you're talking dangerous territory."

"You have the contacts or not?" I said.

"Yes, Michael," he said. "Tell me what you want. Now. Or I'm hanging up."

"I think we found the men who shot Frank Marshall," I said.

"I'm listening," Stern said.

I told Lenny what I needed. About the passports and Pellston airport. About airline tickets and phony names.

"All right, Michael," Stern said. "Let me see what I can do. Got to drive to Grand Rapids in the morning. It'll be later in the day. You understand that?"

"Yes."

"Don't call me back, Michael," he said. "I'll call you."

"Okay," I said. "And, Lenny?"

"Yeah."

"Email the passport photos, will ya," I said. "We have to ID the right guys."

"Jesus Christ," he said and the line went dead.

I put the phone down and looked at AJ and Henri.

"Now what?" AJ said.

"Now, we wait."

47

"Okay, boss," Sandy said. "Are you gonna pace around the office all day?"

It was late by the time Henri went back to his room at the Perry. I stayed at AJ's, but didn't sleep very well. Too much felt out of control. Were our assumptions about the shooters right? Would Lenny Stern's contacts be willing to help? Would the shooters get out of the country before we got them?

I'd left AJ's early in the morning and took the car home for a shower and fresh clothes. The rain and clouds had given way to a clear, chilly sunrise. A beautiful fall morning for a run, and I didn't even get to walk home. A lot going on. It was going to be a long day.

"Go down to Roast & Toast and get a muffin or something," Sandy said. I was in the front office looking out the window at Lake Street. I'd done that several times this morning.

"Am I bothering you?" I said.

"Yes," Sandy said. "I've got work to do. Work you're paying me good money to do, I might add, but I can't concentrate with you around."

"Thanks a lot."

"You gonna be here long?" she said.

"Henri'll be here in a little while," I said.

"Oh, good," Sandy said. "I get to watch the two of you wear a rut in our nice hardwood floor."

"You got anything for me to do?" I said.

Sandy pushed back from her desk. "What am I going to do with you," she said, shaking her head. "I already told you, Michael. I put three files on your desk. Remember the Winslow divorce? You know, a paying client?"

"I forgot," I said.

"No kidding."

"What about the other two?"

"Nothing urgent like Winslow," she said. "Take care of your clients. It's better than waiting for the phone to ring."

"Get out of your hair's what you really mean, isn't it?"

"Go," Sandy said and pointed. "To your office."

I managed to stay in my office and actually work on the files Sandy had given me. By the time I was through, I'd polished off a Lake Street Salad from Roast & Toast and a bottle of water. I was hungrier than I thought.

I heard the outer door open and a voice said hello to Sandy.

"Come on in, Henri," I said.

He came through the door and sat in the chair on the sidewall, the one Sandy usually takes. She followed him in the office.

"Can I get you anything, Henri?"

He shook his head. "Thanks. I just finished a spinach and feta omelet."

"You in the middle of something?" I said to Sandy.

"Of course," she said. "What do you need?"

"Get some coffee and sit down," I said. "Got a problem we need to solve."

"Be right back," she said and went out.

"Haven't heard from Stern, I take it?" Henri said.

I shook my head. Sandy came back with a mug of coffee and stood in front of my desk.

"What?" I said.

"Well, it's just," she said and hesitated. "It's just that I always sit there," she pointed at the side chair, "when we brainstorm. It's comfortable, I guess."

Before I could say anything, Henri got up.

"I'll trade you," he said. "No big deal."

Sandy sat by the wall and drank some coffee. "That's better," she said and took a deep breath. "I'm ready now, what's the problem?"

I leaned forward on the desk. Coffee would have tasted good, but I was wired enough as it was.

"Let's say Lenny nails the two guys at Audie's as our shooters."

"That'd be good news," Henri said.

"Yes, it would," I said.

"Let's also say that they're flying out of Pellston soon," I said. "Like in a day or two."

"Is that good news or bad?" Sandy said.

"It's good news if they haven't gone yet," I said.

"Is that the problem?" Sandy said. "When they fly out?"

I shook my head. "If Lenny's contact has the passenger list, we'll know the day and time."

"Just tell me the problem," Sandy said.

"The problem," Henri said, "is where are they hiding until the plane takes off?"

"Right," I said. "We can't very well take them at the airport."

"Well, we could," Henri said.

"No, Henri," I said. "No shootouts at the Pellston airport. We find out where they're hiding and take 'em there."

"That's your big problem?" Sandy said. "Where the two guys are hiding?"

"That's it."

She drank some coffee, put the mug on the edge of the desk and smiled. "That's easy."

"It is?" Henri said.

"Un-huh," she said.

"Do tell," I said.

"They're at Kellerman's dump on Levering Road."

I looked over at Henri who looked back at me.

"You mean you hotshots never thought of that?" Sandy waited for a response but none came. "No?" She got out of the chair and picked up her mug. "Geez, you guys oughta be working for me," she said and started for the door.

"Not so fast," I said. "Sit back down in your brainstorming chair."

She sat down but kept her mug in her lap.

"Well?" I said. Really wish I had coffee.

"It's the only place that makes sense," she said. "His house on Pickerel Lake Road is rented. They're not at a public place, a motel, a B&B. They know the cops are looking. Probably know about you, too."

"We're only guessing Kellerman's tied to the gunmen," I said.

"I know that," she said, "but we're betting Kellerman's a link to all of them. We've said it more than once."

"Yeah," I said. "We have."

"I already went by the Levering place, remember?"

I nodded.

"Didn't seem like any one was there," she said, "but it might be good to check again. See if anybody's home. Want me to drive up there?"

"No," I said.

"I'll do it," Henri said.

"It's not easy to see from the road," Sandy said.

"You found it," Henri said.

"I was lucky," Sandy said. "I'll tell you how to find it."

"Okay," Henri said.

"When you gonna go?" I said.

"After dark."

48

I turned on the television. The Tigers were home to play the Yankees, down a game in the American League Championship Series. If Sandy thought I was annoying this afternoon, it's a good thing she wasn't here trying to watch the game. Too edgy. Couldn't sit still. I wandered around, but my apartment was too small for much of that. No call from Lenny Stern. Henri had yet to return from his reconnaissance trip to Levering. Good thing I'm not prone to anxiety attacks.

The outside buzzer chirped. I got up and went to the door.

"Yes?" I said on the intercom.

"It's me," Henri said.

I opened my door and waited. Henri came up the stairs two at a time, went past me and into the kitchen.

"We make some coffee?"

"Sure," I said. "I'll do it. Find out anything?"

Henri pulled out a chair at the table and sat down. I put eight scoops of coffee into the Mr. Coffee, filled the tank and pushed the button.

"Somebody was in trailer," he said. "Lights were on, TV noise."

"How many?"

Henri shrugged. "Not sure. At least one."

"See anybody?"

Henri shook his head. "Couldn't see in. Windows were covered. Nobody in or out."

I took a mug from the cupboard and filled it with coffee. I handed it to Henri and sat down at the table.

"Thanks," he said. "I wandered around a little. Got a feel for the place, terrain around the trailer, that sort of thing. Place is a real dump, all right."

"Nothing of interest around the place?"

Henri shook his head and drank some coffee.

"There was a car. Ford Fusion. Blue? Black, maybe. Couldn't tell." He put the mug on the table.

"Plates?"

"Florida."

"Florida?"

He nodded. "Not much help, I'm afraid."

"Could be an airport rental, I suppose," I said. "Some of those cars travel one way."

"Sure. What's Pellston got?"

"Hertz. Avis, too, I think." I got a glass from the cupboard and filled it with ice and water.

"Know anyone who works there? Might help out?"

I shook my head. "Don't think so," I said. "But there might be another a way."

My phone buzzed on the kitchen counter. I got up.

"It's AJ." I swiped the screen. "Hi, sweetheart."

"Michael," she said. "Will you come over, please?"

She sounded, not upset exactly, but her voice was different somehow, deeper, raspy.

"You okay?"

"Yes," she said, "but come to the house. Now, please."

"Henri's here," I said. "Want him, too?"

"Doesn't matter, but I need you."

"Be right there," I said.

"Michael?"

"Yeah?"

"Drive over. Don't walk."

"Drive?" I said. "I always walk."

"I know you do," she said. "Not this time. Okay?"

"Yes," I said and clicked off.

Henri was pouring more coffee. I told him what AJ said.

"I'll stay here," he said. "AJ might want some privacy. Let me know if you need me."

I nodded, got my coat and slipped my gun out of the holster and into the coat pocket.

"Michael," Henri said. "Keep an eye out. Just in case."

49

The walk to AJ's house takes only minutes if I'm not in a hurry. I was in a hurry, so I got the BMW out of the parking lot, went left on Bay Street and four blocks later, I turned into her driveway. I went to the kitchen door, at the back of the house, as I always do. AJ was waiting for me.

I walked in and kissed her, softly, on the lips.

"Sure you're okay?" I took off my coat and hung it on a rack next to the door.

"Yes," she said, nodding. "Lenny just called."

"Called here?" I said.

AJ nodded.

"What'd he want?"

"Wants you to call him right away," she said. "He's only got a few minutes."

I turned to get the phone out of my jacket pocket.

"No," AJ said. "No cellphone. Lenny was very clear. Landline only."

"Think he called here 'cuz I don't have a landline?"

AJ nodded. "You call on your cell, he won't answer."

"He say what this was about?"

AJ shook her head. "No, but I'll bet it has something to do with the passports." She pointed to a white cordless phone tucked in next to a stainless toaster on the kitchen counter. "Call," she said.

I picked up the phone.

"Here," AJ said and handed me a pencil and a slip of paper with Lenny's number. It wasn't his cell.

"You know where he is?"

"Didn't say."

I punched the number. He picked up on the first ring.

"Lenny?"

"Have to make this quick, Michael," he said.

"I'm on AJ's phone at the house."

"I know," he said.

"Where are you?"

"Never mind that," he said.

"You think a cell call'd be monitored?"

"Not taking any chances," he said.

"Okay."

"Got a few ground rules first."

"Okay."

"Non-negotiable. Agreed?"

"Agreed," I said.

"We never talk about this call again. Agreed?"

"Yes."

"You do not have my permission to say where the information came from. Agreed? I'm not your source on this."

"Agreed."

"Is AJ there?"

"Yes."

"Put me on speaker phone."

I punched a button on the base unit. "Can you hear me, Lenny?" I said.

"Yeah," he said. "You there, AJ?"

"Right here, Lenny."

"AJ, this comes together, I get it for the print edition first. Deal?"

"Online could get it up earlier," she said.

"Not good enough," Stern said.

I rapped my knuckles on the kitchen counter and put my hands together like I was praying. I mouthed the word, "please."

"If I get it up first, you still get the by-line. How's that?"

"Good enough," he said. "Michael?"

"Right here."

Lenny coughed twice and cleared his throat.

"Two men with U.S. passports. Just issued. Rush service." He coughed again. "The applications were hand delivered to the agency office on Dearborn Street. Not unheard of, but unusual."

"Give me the names." He did and I wrote them down.

"You think these are my guys?" I said.

"You tell me," Lenny said. "Same guys are booked on Delta out of Pellston." I gave AJ a thumbs-up sign. She nodded.

"They going to Europe?" I said.

"Narita."

"Tokyo?"

"Un-huh," he said.

"Must be my guys," I said.

"I emailed the photos. Should be in your box right now."

"Good."

"Delete 'em when you're done, okay?"

"Sure," I said. "Do you know when they leave Pellston?"

"First thing in the morning."

"Tomorrow?"

"Tomorrow," he said. "Six-twenty. Out of Detroit in the afternoon."

My head was spinning. We'd caught a break, but it went straight to fast forward.

"Thanks, Lenny. I appreciate your help."

"Hope so," he said. "Called in a few on this one."

"Okay. Thanks, really."

"One more thing," he said. "Don't know if it'll help, but a man with one of the passport names rented a car at O'Hare. Still logged out. A blue Ford with Florida plates."

"Holy shit," I said. "That nails it, Lenny. The car . . ."

"I don't want to know, Michael. Don't tell me until I can use the whole thing. Look, I'm late. Good luck."

The line went dead before I had a chance to say anything else.

"It's them," AJ said.

"Got to be," I said. "Your printer working?"

"Sure," she said.

I turned and went out of the kitchen to AJ's office on the other side of the living room. It had been a small back porch at one time, but AJ converted it to an office when she remodeled the house a few years ago. It had windows on three sides, which gave the room a larger, more open feel.

She followed me into the office.

"Okay?" I said, pointing at the Mac laptop on the desk.

"Of course."

I sat down, opened the lid and waited. I found the email from Lenny and clicked on the attachments. Two photos appeared on the screen.

"The Mexican and the black," AJ said. "As Pam Wiecek would say."

"Yep."

I hit a button and the printer came to life on a small table next to the desk. I picked up the photos and went back to the kitchen table. I sat down to text Henri.

"Back in a minute. Tell you then." I pushed send.

In a moment, my iPhone chirped. "On the right track?" Henri wrote.

I tapped out, "yes" and clicked off my phone.

"Sandy was right about Levering, after all," she said. "Helluva guess."

"Educated guess is more like it," I said. "Smart woman."

We sat at the table and were quiet. AJ reached over and took my hand. "You told Henri you'd be right back," she said. "You should get going."

I nodded. AJ squeezed my hand.

"You're going after them, aren't you," she said.

I nodded slowly.

"Tonight."

"Yes."

"Would it do me any good to tell you to call the cops?"

I shook my head. "No."

"Sure?"

"We've been over this," I said. "Nothing to tell them anyway. We're guessing with Kellerman dead."

"Educated guessing."

"Not enough for the cops."

"But it doesn't matter, does it?" she said.

"What doesn't?"

"You want to get them yourself."

I nodded. "Yes," I said.

"You and Henri."

"Yes."

AJ stood up. "Then you better get going," she said.

50

"It's got to be tonight," Henri said. "If they leave Pellston . . ." He turned his palms up and shrugged. "That's it."

We sat in my kitchen. Henri had put a fresh pot of coffee on while I was gone. I got a mug from the cupboard and poured some.

"You want to see if Wiecek'll confirm the photos?" Henri said.

"Un-huh," I said. "I know it's them, but I got to be sure." I picked up my phone and punched Wiecek's number. I drank some coffee and waited.

"Hello, Michael," she said.

"Hi, Pam. Did I catch you at a bad time?"

"I'm fine," she said. "Off tonight."

"I need to talk."

"Go ahead. You know how it is in the fall. Even Audie's slows down."

"I'm sure it does," I said. "Listen, Pam, the two men in the bar that night. One guy had a gun. Remember?"

"Of course I do," she said. "You find them?"

"Think so," I said. "Pam, if I text you two photos, would you take a look and see if it's the same men?"

"Sure," she said.

"Okay to do it now?"

"Sure."

"Take a look and call me right back. Can you do that?"

"Sure can," she said. "After what you did for my sister, I'm happy to help."

I put her number on the photos and hit send. I didn't have to wait long.

"Pam?"

"It's them, Michael," she said.

"Positive?"

"Oh, yes," she said, "I'm positive."

"Thank you, Pam," I said. "Have a pleasant evening off."

I clicked the phone and put it on the table.

"Feel better?" Henri said.

I nodded and picked up my coffee mug. It was empty, so I put it down. "Just wanted to be sure," I said. I looked at Henri. "How we gonna do this?"

"Seems pretty straightforward to me," he said. "But let me think a bit. Make some notes, maybe a drawing."

"That how you'd do it in Iraq?" I said. "Map it out?"

Henri stretched his arms above his head and let out a long, slow breath. He folded his arms across his chest and smiled. A small but discernible smile.

"No," he said, shaking his head. "We'd toss a couple of grenades, be done with it."

"Blow the trailer up?"

He nodded. "Not worth getting killed, there's a safer way."

"What if it's the wrong people inside?"

"Not worth getting killed to find out," he said. "If we're certain enough."

"You're not suggesting . . ."

Henri put his hand up to stop me in mid-sentence.

"Of course not," he said. "This is different."

"Good to hear."

"One thing is certain though," he said.

"What's that?"

"We hit 'em before dawn."

51

"It's time."

I looked at my watch. Just after four. We hadn't slept. Not that I expected to. I left my coffee mug on the counter and went for my coat. I put a box of shells in a side pocket. One last time, I pulled the .38 from my hip holster and checked the cylinder.

Henri took one last drink of coffee and got up. He put his coat on and we went outside.

The night was quiet and a bright moon put light in the sky. An easy breeze drifted up from the Bay, moving leaves at the top of the trees. The air was cold. A few flurries drifted around us in the parking lot as we went to my car. A blanket of snow could surprise us before Halloween.

"Be right there," Henri said and went to his truck parked on the street.

He came back with a good-sized green nylon duffel bag.

He opened the back door put the bag on the seat.

I started the 335. Henri got in and I locked the doors.

"What's in the bag?"

"Running gear," Henri said. "In case I get the chance for a fast five miles."

"Smart-ass."

He ignored me. "How many BMWs we gonna find in Levering?"

"None."

"A little obvious, don't you think?"

"Faster get-a-way," I said.

"Now who's the smart-ass."

I went over to Mitchell then took Division to U.S. 31 north. We moved easily in the light traffic, but I kept it close to the speed limit. Didn't want to attract cops. Not tonight.

I slowed for the stoplight at M-68 in Alanson. It was clear at Pellston, too, as we passed the airport. After twenty minutes, we arrived at Levering. I down-shifted twice and turned east on C-66, the Levering Road.

"How far," I said.

"Not far," Henri said. "Off to the right just short of the Cheboygan County line. Dirt road. Trailer's about one-hundred fifty, two-hundred feet off the road."

I flipped on the Xenon brights. They lit up the shoulders of the road.

"You're sure?" I said.

"I'm sure," Henri said. "Paid close attention when I was here. Wanted to get it right."

"It's really a trailer?"

"Yep," he said. "On cement blocks. Straight out of the fifties."

We rode quietly. Interlochen classical music played softly, but we weren't listening.

"There," he said. "Post on the right. With the mailbox."

"See it."

I came down to second gear, cut the lights and turned in. The car dropped sharply onto a two-track. Dirt and stones scraped the bottom of floor pan.

"You see okay?"

"Okay enough to get us near the trailer," I said.

"A little farther," Henri said, "then we'll walk."

I stopped the 335 and turned it off. LaCroix reached over the seat back and grabbed his duffel bag. He put it in his lap, unzipped it and carefully took out two shotguns.

"Jesus, Henri."

He handed me one of the guns. I took it.

"The hell is this for?"

"Killing people, Russo."

"You gonna start a war?" I said.

"Keep them from starting one," Henri said.

"How do you use this thing?" I said, staring at the cut-down gun.

"Just pull the trigger," he said. "It's a Benelli semi-automatic. Spray and pray."

"You learn that line in Iraq?" I said.

"Nah. Cops taught me that one."

"It's your call," I said. "What's next?"

"I'll go to the right . . ."

Lights. Bright lights. In front of us. Headlights and two spotlights, high up. Probably a truck.

"Get low in your seat," Henri said.

"Shit," I said.

"You can say that again."

"Not what I meant. Lights behind us. We're blocked in."

Henri looked over his shoulder then turned back.

"Let's wait," he said as he chambered a round in the shotgun.

"Wait for what?"

"See what happens."

We sat quietly. No place to go. Even if I could move the car, it'd get stuck on the rough ground.

Nothing happened. Two minutes, maybe three.

The passenger door of the truck in front of us opened and a lone figure stepped out. Henri slipped out of his coat without taking his eyes off the truck. He moved his back holster around to his hip.

The figure moved into the headlights. It was a man. His face was hidden in the shadow of the lights. He walked slowly towards us. His arms were spread wide, wing-like, away from his sides.

"Hit the lights," Henri said. I did. The man stopped. His arms moved slowly and he opened both sides of his coat and held it open. He moved forward again, coat still open. Into our headlights.

"For crissake, Joey DeMio."

"Un-huh," Henri said. "Let's get out. Do it easy. Keep the gun at your side but make sure he sees it."

We opened the car doors and came out easy and slow. DeMio stopped. We went into our headlights and walked towards him. We stopped twenty feet apart. DeMio let go of his coat and put his hands down.

"Joey," I said. "Fancy meeting you here."

He ignored me. "Time to talk."

"So talk," I said.

"Alone."

Henri didn't move.

"Put your guns on the ground, gentlemen."

For a moment, neither Henri nor I moved.

"Cicci's got you sighted," he said. "Put them down."

I leaned over and let my shotgun fall to the road.

"You, too, hot-shot," DeMio said.

Henri didn't move.

"Cicci'll blow your head off, you make a move. Put it on the ground, LaCroix. Get back in the car."

"Henri," I said.

"Not good, Russo," he said.

"What are you worried about, soldier boy," DeMio said. "If I wanted you dead, you'd be on the ground already." DeMio buttoned his coat and turned up his collar. "Want to talk to the counselor here."

"It's all right, Henri," I said.

Henri hesitated but put the shotgun down and went to the car, walking backwards all the way.

"You protecting killers now, Joey?" I said, pointing to the trailer.

DeMio walked up to me.

"They're dead, counselor."

"What?" I said. I looked at the trailer then back at Joey. "Dead?"

"Both of 'em. It's over. My debt is paid."

"It wasn't your debt, Joey."

"Bullshit," he said. "We knew, you and me. The day you came for a favor."

"But this," I said, pointing at the trailer again. "Why?"

"You don't kill people, counselor, I kill people. It's done. My debt is paid."

"What about Phil Morgan?"

"He's out of it," DeMio said. "Told you that already."

"He ordered the hit."

"This is Baldini family business," he said. "I guaranteed Morgan's safety. Forget him."

"Not sure I like that," I said.

"Not about what you like, counselor," DeMio said. "It's the price you pay. The two in there," he gestured at the trailer, "are dead. Cops'll know they got the right guys."

"Cops're going to ask a lot of questions," I said. "Probably start with me."

"Your problem, counselor," DeMio said. "But let me make something clear. A cop says one word to me about these guys," he gestured over his shoulder, "I'm comin' for you."

"You threatening me, Joey?"

DeMio nodded slowly.

"What if Morgan comes after Frank again?" I said. "Or me?"

Joey shook his head. "Won't happen. He swore to forgo the revenge," he said. "Morgan's out. Understand?"

Of course I understood. Tough to swallow, that's all.

I nodded.

DeMio raised his arm and waved it from side to side. The car at the end of the drive started its motor, edged slowly backwards and disappeared.

"One more thing," I said.

"What's that?"

"Kellerman."

"The lawyer?"

"You ace him, too?"

DeMio shrugged. "He stepped over the line."

"Sending guys to rough me up?" I said. "Too much attention in a small town. Is that it?"

"Smart guy, counselor," DeMio said. "Wasting your time on divorces. You could do better."

"Carmine said the same thing to me once."

"I remember," DeMio said, smiling. "Go on, get out. You have no business here."

I turned around, collected both shotguns, and walked to the car. I looked back but Joey had disappeared behind the lights of the truck. I put the guns on the back seat, got in and closed the door.

"Let's get outta here," I said.

I slowly backed the car down the driveway, up onto Levering Road and headed towards 31.

Henri pulled a cell phone out of his pocket and punched a few keys.

"Who you calling?" I said.

"Sheriff."

"On your cell?"

"It's a throw-a-way," Henri said. "Time to do my civic duty."

52

We sat in my office. I leaned back in my chair with my hands behind my head. Henri sat in the client chair with his feet on the edge of the desk. It was a little after nine. We'd been there a while. We hadn't said much to each other. Sandy was surprised to find us there when she arrived for work.

"I put more coffee on," Sandy said. "Done in a minute."

"Thanks," I said.

"You do look like you been up all night," she said.

"That's because we been up all night," Henri said.

"Always the mouth," Sandy said shaking her head. She sat down in her usual chair. I filled her in on the evening's trip to Levering.

"Let me see if I got this straight," Sandy said. "Everything went through Joey DeMio. Is that right?"

I nodded.

"This Mafia guy in Chicago. What's his name again?"

"Phil Morgan."

"Okay, Morgan asked Joey to kill Frank," she said, "so Joey got Kellerman and told him to hire the two shooters from L.A. . . ."

"Kellerman was the buffer between the L.A. shooters and DeMio," I said.

"The L.A. guys shot Frank and hid out while they waited for passports," Sandy said.

"But Michael's snooping around made DeMio and Kellerman nervous," Henri said, "so Kellerman hired the dropouts to scare Michael off."

"That didn't work out so well," Sandy said.

Henri shook his head. "Especially after Kellerman sent the kids a second time."

"When Henri shot Kevin Gayles," I said, "DeMio knew Kellerman had gone too far, so he had him killed."

Sandy folded her arms across her chest and shook her head. "I don't know," she said. "There are some nasty people in our corner of the world."

"Not just in the big, bad cities," I said.

"We think we're different up here," Sandy said, "but . . ."

The outer door opened and Sandy stopped talking. We heard steps and Martin Fleener appeared at my door.

"You don't look so good," Sandy said. "Want coffee?"

Fleener shook his head. "Had enough, thanks," he said and came into the office.

"Close the door on your way out, Sandy. Please." It wasn't a request. It was an order, politely delivered. Sandy got up and went for the door.

"Holler if you want anything," she said and left.

Fleener took off his coat, a dark khaki Burberry, put it over the back of the client chair on the sidewall and sat down. He moved the chair out and tipped it back to lean against the wall. Fleener let out a big, noticeable sigh.

"You guys're in a bit early, aren't you?" he said.

"Rise and shine," Henri said with a grin.

"Early bird and all that," I said.

Fleener nodded. "You could use a shave, Henri."

"Got a job," he said. "Model in a photo shoot."

"He needed a more contemporary look," I said and smiled.

Fleener looked straight ahead. He moved forward and the chair came down on the wood floor hard. And loud.

"You want to play Butch Cassidy and the Sundance Kid, do it to somebody else. I'm tired and too cranky." Fleener tilted the chair back against the wall again.

"Got two dead guys up in Levering," he said. "Know anything about that?" He stared straight ahead, not at either of us.

"Sorry," Henri said, "can't help you."

"What about you?" he said to me without looking my way.

"Why do you think we know about dead guys in Levering?"

"Oh, I don't know," he said, slowly, sarcastically. "Found some interesting stuff at the house."

"Such as?" I asked.

"Such as two handguns. In plastic bags on the kitchen table." Fleener looked at me. "Know anything about that?"

I shook my head.

Fleener's eyes moved to Henri. "How about you?"

Henri shrugged.

"Okay, okay," Fleener said, "have it your way." He let the chair down, easily this time. He got up, picked up his coat and went for the door.

"Be in Hendricks' office at one-thirty. Both of you."

Fleener put on his coat. He nodded and said good-bye to Sandy on the way out.

Sandy came to the door. She leaned against the doorjamb holding a mug of coffee.

"Would his visit have anything to do with news reports about dead men in Levering?" she said.

"You listening through the door?" I said.

"Of course," she said.

"What'd the news say?"

"Not much," Sandy said. "Cops found the men in a house in Levering. They're investigating. That's it."

Sandy came off the doorjamb and drank some coffee. "Think the cops know the dead guys are the shooters?"

I shrugged. "We meet with Hendricks this afternoon," I said. "Let you know after that?"

"Yeah," she said and went back to her desk.

"Want some breakfast?" Henri said.

I shook my head. "I got time to run up to Cherokee Point. Want to tell Frank and Ellen it's over."

"Be good to hear it from you," Henri said.

"I'll meet you back here," I said. "We need to talk about what we'll say to Hendricks."

Henri shook his head. "We don't need to talk about that at all."

"And why not?"

"We say nothing. We plead ignorance."

"Hendricks and Fleener aren't that dumb, Henri. Marty sat right there." I pointed at the side chair. "He knows we're involved."

"But not how we're involved," Henri said, "unless we tell them." Henri got out of his chair. "Can't prove a thing, we don't help 'em."

"Not sure about that, I guess."

"Be sure, Michael."

53

"I'm glad it's over," Ellen said. "It's like I can breathe again."

I sat with Frank and Ellen at the table in their kitchen. We drank coffee. I picked at a plate of scrambled eggs and toast Frank fixed while I told them what happened in Levering.

"You seem confident that Phil Morgan won't come after Frank, or you, for that matter."

I nodded. "Morgan gave his word to Joey, Ellen, not me."

"If he's anything like his old man," Frank said, "he'll keep his word." Frank drank some coffee. "Besides, if Phil Morgan comes after either of us, we won't worry for very long. Joey'd kill him."

"The only thing that would have been better, Michael, is if you'd killed them. Or Henri."

"I know," I said. "If it'd been necessary . . ."

"But it wasn't necessary," Frank said. "It's all right with me that Joey had them killed."

"You ever kill anyone, Frank?" I said. "All those years in Chicago."

Frank shook his head. "Closest I came was when I was still a young beat cop." He smiled. "God that was a long time ago."

"What happened?"

"Guy ran out of a liquor store one night. I walked by just as the owner came out the door yelling for help. Chased the guy. He cut up an alley and I followed him. He spun around, took a shot at me. I dropped to the ground, pulled my gun. The guy tried to run, but he tripped on something. Hit his head. He was still out cold when the ambulance got there."

"You didn't even fire your gun?"

"Nope," Frank said. "All these years, I'm still happy I didn't have to shoot."

"But you were ready to?"

"Sure," he said. "It was my job."

"Remember when we used to talk about that, Frank?" Ellen said. "Especially those first couple of years at Winckler, Norton and Barger?"

Frank nodded. "Yeah."

"It was harder to pull a gun when you were an investigator," Ellen said. "We had plenty late night talks about that."

"I'm missing something," I said. "You were trained as an officer. Didn't that help you?"

"The line seemed clearer when I was a cop, Michael." He looked over at Ellen. She smiled at him. "I thought about it a lot more when I didn't have a badge."

"But you were ready to pull your gun if you had to?"

Frank nodded. "But that's not the same as being comfortable with the idea."

"I'm struggling with some of this," I said.

"About using a gun?" Ellen said.

I nodded. "Yeah."

"Welcome to the club," Frank said. "Call me anytime, Michael. If you think I can help."

"Thanks," I said.

We chatted for a few minutes, but it was time to get back to town. I didn't want to be late for my meeting at the prosecutor's office.

54

"I'd like a cup of coffee," I said to Don Hendricks.

"You won't be here long enough to enjoy it, Mr. Russo," he said. He drank coffee from a large ceramic mug that read "Petoskey Northmen" on the side. Hendricks sat hunched over his desk. Papers and folders were stacked five inches high on his left next to the office phone. His screen and keyboard were to his right. He pushed his right sleeve up, moved the mouse around its pad and clicked several times. I couldn't tell if he was ignoring Henri and me or prepping for us.

Martin Fleener was tastefully tailored in a navy three-piece suit with a solid maroon tie over a white shirt. He sat in his usual chair with neither coffee nor water. He still wore his suit jacket. Guess he didn't think this meeting was going to last very long either.

Henri and I sat in the dull metal chairs in front of Hendricks' desk. I had absolutely no idea how long the meeting would last. Not that it mattered much.

Hendricks clicked the mouse one last time, took a green folder off the top of the stack and put it in front of him. He looked up at me, then at Henri, and opened the folder. He leaned forward, his forearms on the folder.

"There's too much killing in my county," he said.

"We did not kill anyone," Henri said, emphasizing the "we."

Hendricks arm came up from the desk and he pointed at Henri. "Shut up, Mr. LaCroix," he said. "You, both of you, are here to listen."

Henri said nothing. Neither did I. Seemed no point.

Hendricks sat back in his chair. He moved his mug away from the files.

"It'll come as no surprise to you, gentlemen, that we have two more bodies on our hands. Sheriff got an anonymous tip about five this morning."

"Deputies went to Levering to take a look, called Marty." Hendricks nodded Fleener's way. "Marty called me."

Hendricks shuffled some papers from the file. "You won't be surprised either, the dead men were the perps who shot Frank Marshall." He paused for a moment. "But I bet you would be surprised to know we have the evidence to prove it."

"Evidence?" I said.

"Thought I'd get you on that one," Hendricks said.

I gestured at Fleener. "Marty said you had guns."

Hendricks nodded. "Got a rush test this morning. Ballistics confirmed the handguns as the weapons used to shoot Frank Marshall."

"Where'd you find the guns?" I said.

Hendricks smiled but it wasn't a happy smile. "Well," he said, "that's where things got interesting." Hendricks looked over at Fleener.

"I got there first," Fleener said. "Patrol officers waited for me. Crime scene people, too. Didn't touch a thing."

I shrugged. "That's not unusual," I said, "wait for you to see the bodies."

Fleener shook his head. "No," he said. "It's what else they found that had everyone unusually cautious."

I had no idea where he was headed with this one. Crime scenes often had a sameness to them. So did procedure.

"Don came in a few minutes after I did," Fleener said.

"I'll tell you what we found, Mr. Russo," Hendricks said.

I was tempted to tell him to get on with it and not string it out, but I kept my mouth shut.

"Better yet, would you like to know my reaction when I walked into that dump?" Hendricks said in a flat voice.

"Yes," I said, keeping it simple.

"Like I'd walked into the evidence room," he said. "It was all there waiting for us. Like we'd called ahead."

"What d'ya mean?" I said, not at all sure what he meant.

"It was all there," Hendricks said, "on the kitchen table. Two handguns, each neatly wrapped in a plastic bag." He coughed. "Two passports. And how 'bout this? The pictures in the passports? They matched the faces of the dead guys on the floor."

"What killed them?" I said.

"Small caliber bullet in the back of the head," Fleener said. "Probably a .22. Very professional."

"We also found a receipt for two plane tickets. Guess who?"

I knew it was a rhetorical question.

"The names on the passports," Hendricks said. "Our dead guys were ticketed from Pellston to Tokyo."

Hendricks stopped and scratched his forehead. He glanced at Henri.

"Any of this familiar to you, Mr. LaCroix?"

Henri shook his head. "Nope."

"Didn't think so," Hendricks said. "What about you?" he said to me.

"News to me," I said. He didn't believe us. No point trying to convince him of that.

Hendricks ignored my response.

"Here's something else I bet you didn't know, gentlemen," Hendricks said. "We ran their prints. We ignored the phony names, of course."

Hendricks sorted through papers in the file and found the sheets he was looking for.

"Ronaldo Olivera, born twenty-eight years ago in Durango."

"Mexico?" I said.

Hendricks nodded.

Wonder if Pam Wiecek'd be surprised to know that?

"Known to his friends as 'Ronnie the Rat.' Charming. Got a Green Card three years ago. Been arrested a few times in L.A. No charges. No obvious mob connections."

Hendricks picked up the other sheet.

"DeMarcus Jackson, born eighteen years ago in Oakland, California. Several priors. Worked his way up from small time robberies to enforcer. Says here he was pretty good with a gun."

Hendricks closed the folder and put it back on the stack of papers. He picked up his mug and drank some coffee.

"What we don't have is a motive. Why'd they try to assassinate Frank Marshall?"

"Probably hired to do the job, don't you think?"

Hendricks nodded. "I do think," he said. "But I don't know why they were hired. Can you help us out with that, gentlemen?"

Henri shook his head. "Sorry."

"Wish I could help, Don," I said.

Hendricks fist hit the desk. Hard. "Bullshit," he said. "You don't want to help. That's all. You don't want to."

Hendricks sat back in his chair and folded his heavy arms across his chest.

"The killing's going to stop, gentlemen. Do I make myself clear?"

"I told you before," Henri said. "We didn't kill anyone."

Hendricks came forward and his arms landed on the desk. "And I told you before, you're here to listen."

I started to say something, but Hendricks put an index finger in the air and waved me off.

"We'll test your guns because we have to do that," he said, "but it'll only confirm what we already know. You didn't kill 'em. But you know who did. I'd bet on that." Hendricks hesitated for a moment. "If I were really a betting man, I'd put a hundred on our friend on Mackinac Island."

Henri was quiet. Me, too.

Hendricks took in a lot of air and let it out, slowly. He looked over at Fleener. "Got anything to add, Marty?" he said.

Fleener shook his head. "No, thanks, Don," he said. "You covered it."

Hendricks got out of his chair, came around and leaned on the front edge of his desk.

"All right," he said. "We got the gunmen who shot up our streets. Hooray for us. The *Post Dispatch* will have a big story. The city fathers will be all smiles. They'll call to congratulate us. Nobody'll care there's another shooter out there. Who cares if they shoot each other, they'll say."

Hendricks eased himself onto the desk and sat there. He looked over at Fleener then back at us.

"Here's the way it's gonna be," he said. "Don't ever get into anything like this again. Understand?"

He didn't give us a chance to respond.

"You're shielding killers is what you're doing," he said. "That's the part I don't like. Nobody'll miss those guys in the trailer. Killing was a way of life for them. Would have happened sooner or later. But I don't like unsolved murders in Emmet County. And I especially don't like it when guys I know, guys who ought to know better, play vigilante in my county."

Hendricks got off the desk and stood in front of Henri and me. Only a few feet away.

"I'll let it go," he said. "This time. Can't prove you were involved anyway. Do anything like this again, I'll fucking come after both of you. And I'll make it stick. Got it?"

Henri nodded.

"Not good enough," Hendricks said. "I'd especially enjoy coming after you, LaCroix. You understand, or not?"

"I do," Henri said.

"Russo?"

"I understand."

"Good," he said. "Now get out."

55

"**D**o you think Hendricks'll figure out Joey DeMio killed the L.A. guys?" AJ said.

We sat on the couch in front of the fireplace. The logs burned with a soft flame. It was getting colder outside. A light dusting of snow covered the grass, but the streets were still clear. I got to AJ's before she arrived home from the paper, planning to do an easy run. I put on my light winter gear and stood in the living room window while I stretched. I watched AJ pull into the drive and suddenly a run didn't seem as appealing anymore. I put my hat and gloves away and met her at the backdoor.

AJ changed into the sloppiest pair of sweatpants I'd seen on her in a long time. She put on a brown rag wool sweater that hung out over the top of the pants. I still wore my running gear. We sipped Chardonnay, chewed Cashews from a ceramic bowl on the coffee table, and held hands.

"Michael? Did you hear my question?"

"Sorry," I said. "Yeah, I did. Just thinking about something else. Sorry."

"Will Hendricks find out about Joey?"

I nodded. "Sooner or later," I said. "Be surprised he could prove it though."

"He could have made things much tougher for you and Henri," AJ said and picked up her glass.

"Yes, he could have," I said. "If he'd wanted to."

"Think he'll stay pissed at you?"

I smiled. "He'll get over it," I said. "Sooner rather than later."

I picked up my glass and raised it to AJ's.

"What're we toasting?"

"Us," I said, emphatically.

"I love you," she said and leaned over and kissed me.

"Me, too," I said and smiled.

I took a few Cashews and popped them in my mouth one at a time.

"What were you thinking about a minute ago?" AJ said. "When I asked about DeMio?"

"Oh, I don't know," I said. "Just a feeling." I hesitated. "It's hard to pin down."

"Would it have anything to do with going after the shooters?"

"I've gone after bad guys before," I said.

"Yeah, but this was different."

I drank some wine and thought about that.

"You weren't simply defending yourself," she said.

"No."

"It was more than that," she said.

"Yes."

AJ took my hand and kissed it softly. When she put it back down, she did not let go.

"I wanted to get them. I would have killed them myself, if it came to that."

"You think it would have come to that?"

I nodded. "Yes," I said. "They'd never have let us take 'em."

"Are you okay with that?" she said.

"Killing them myself?"

AJ nodded.

I took a deep breath. "Yes."

"Is that what bothers you," she said, "that you would have killed them or that you decided that killing them was acceptable?"

"Interesting distinction," I said. "Can you imagine us having this conversation a couple of years ago?"

"Things have changed," AJ said.

I poured wine into my glass and offered AJ some. She shook her head.

"Henri said I'd moved into a different world."

"A world where killing is both possible and acceptable?" she said.

"Yeah," I said. I looked at AJ. "At least I didn't have to find out last night."

"There'll be a next time, you know," she said. "You'll find out next time."

"I know."

AJ put down her glass and moved closer. She put her head on my shoulder and I put my arm around her.

The fire had burned down. I wanted to put on another log. But not right now.

ACKNOWLEDGEMENTS

Like the first Michael Russo mystery, *Murder at Cherokee Point*, I made it all up. The story should not remind you of real people or events. If it does, perhaps I have given all my characters, especially Michael, AJ, and Henri, more realistic, fuller lives this time around. Several people helped me make the story more believable and more enjoyable. They include Frances Barger, Mary Jane Barnwell, Marietta Hamady, Tanya Hartman, Jay Jones, Wesley Maurer, Jr., Marta J. Olson, Aaron Stander, and Chris West. The Mystery Writing Workshop at the Interlochen Center for the Arts kept me motivated and pushed me to get better at creating suspense. Summer is such a pleasant time to spend a few days on campus. The writers around our table offered lots of encouragement and support to finish the novel. What a delightful group.

Heather Shaw, editor extraordinaire, did it again. Her critique, even when I grumbled while reading it, made the writing better, clearer and more interesting.

Ray Elkins, Sheriff of Cedar County, Michigan, appeared through the courtesy of Aaron Stander, author of the Ray Elkins Thriller series. Sheriff Elkins wanted me to tell readers that the food at the Cedar County jail is pretty darn good.

PETER MARABELL

Peter Marabell grew up in metro Detroit, spending as much time as possible street racing on Woodward Avenue in the 1950s and visiting the Straits of Mackinac. With a Ph.D. in History and Politics, Peter spent most of his professional career on the faculty at Michigan State University. He is the author of the historic monograph, *Frederick Libby and the American Peace Movement*. His first novel, *More than a Body*, was published in 2013, and the first of the Michael Russo mystery series, *Murder at Cherokee Point*, was published in 2014. As a freelance writer, he worked in several professional fields including healthcare, politics, and the arts. In 2002, Peter moved permanently to Northern Michigan with his spouse and business partner, Frances Barger, to live, write, and work at their businesses on Mackinac Island. All things considered, he would rather obsess about American politics, or Spartan basketball, after a good five-mile run on the hills of Mackinac Island.

OTHER BOOKS BY PETER MARABELL

More than a Body

Murder at Cherokee Point

also

Frederick Libby and the American Peace Movement

Made in the USA
Middletown, DE
05 June 2016